MW01487257

Copyright © 2018 by Jud Widing

Cover artwork by Scott Siskind
www.scottsiskind.com

All rights reserved. This book or any portion thereof may not be
reproduced or used in any manner whatsoever without the express
written permission of the publisher except for the use of brief
quotations in a book review.

La Reudugier originally appeared on *Storgy*
Goosin' Bruiser originally appeared in Vol. 78 of *Suspense Magazine*
Hazards originally appeared in Vol. 5.4 of *Star 82 Review*
Takers originally appeared in Vol. 18 of *The Offbeat*

Designed by Jud Widing
Edited by Gene Christopher

www.judwiding.com
Facebook/Twitter/Instagram: @judwiding

IDENTICAL PIGS

Stories by

Jud Widing

TABLE OF CONTENTS

And then there's a bunch of just really terrific little
jokes in between all of those. You'll see.

Two pigs alike in shape and size
Like all the pigs the butcher buys
But in the end one grows more wise
By watching how the other dies

AUTHOR'S NOTE

Some of these stories have been published before. Some haven't. All, however, have been re-edited for this collection. In as much as this matters to anyone, the versions of the stories presented here can be considered "definitive".

LA REUDUGIER

Rachel had told Loretta that her boyfriend Barry's friend Arnold was tall and handsome and also nice, which was good enough for Loretta at the time of the telling, when she had been lying prostrate on Rachel's bed, kicking her mismatched socks in the air, tracing lazy rainbows over the algebra problems they'd solved incorrectly or not at all.

"He's a wrestler," Rachel added with a wink.

Loretta smiled at the innuendo she recognized but didn't understand. "Oooh." The smile collapsed into a grimace. "Does that mean he spits into a bottle?"

Rachel laughed at her mathematics. "What?"

"Wrestlers have to make weight, so they stop drinking water and then they spit in a bottle."

Silence, broken only by the *scrrchscrrchscrrch* of martyred graphite, gripped Rachel's bedroom. That was when Loretta had known something was up. Rachel was a connoisseur of all things nasty; no way she'd hear about hunks dribbling into empty Gatorade bottles and not hypothesize a next step for the expectorations.

Finally, Rachel laid her pencil gently onto her notebook, as though trying not to wake it. "Well," she said, "do you want to ask him?"

"He's a wrestler," Loretta echoed with an absolute minimum of winking. Her tone contained a treatise on the social hierarchy of Herkimer Jr./Sr. High School, imparting knowledge gained through extensive experience and at great personal expense.

And so Rachel parried with a disquisition of her own, this one largely devoid of subtext. Rachel's boyfriend Barry's friend Arnold was not only tall and handsome and also nice, but *also* also interested in Loretta, which was why Rachel had mentioned him in the first place. If Loretta was interested in Arnold, Rachel could tell Barry to tell Arnold that Loretta told Rachel that she, being Loretta, was interested in him, i.e. Arnold. And then they would go on a date, and then maybe they would fall in love and be sexual and get a house and have kids and support each other's bad habits and die in each other's arms.

The social anthropologist in Loretta swirled a glass of sherry and shook her head. *No no,* she scoffed, *that simply isn't possible. Arnold is popular and eighteen. You're worse than unpopular, you're un-popular, lacking the requisite distinction to be a true pariah.* Swirl swirl. *Not to mention, you're sixteen.*

Never one to side with drink-swirlers, Loretta agreed immediately, not with reason but with fancy, and that agreement crackled its way along the twenty-first century grapevine, far less direct than the old zip through the phone line but altogether quicker. Rachel pecked "Loretta says yes!!" into her phone and hit send, at which point the message shot to the top of the antennae at the nearest cell site (which was over in Bucks county), where it was processed by some brilliant little robots and punted to a mobile switching center, where yet another battery of helpful automatons fell upon the announcement of assent with generous, inhuman ministrations, concluding by flinging the data to the IMS core of Rachel's provider, where a machine that had been flirting with self-awareness for a frighteningly long period of time (but fortunately hadn't found the right pick-up lines yet) assessed the message, found it pointless, and shot-putted it back through the entire chain in reverse, except this time to Barry's phone. All of this happened in an instant, which was how much time seemed to pass before Loretta was *here*, in the La Reudugier, trying to figure out which one was Arnold.

Tall, handsome and also nice. Yes, that had been sufficient in Rachel's room, when it had just been two girls talking. But La Reudugier, one of those trendy coffee spots with an ostentatious exposed-wood façade and a sign that would spell Here Comes Gentrification if only they could afford enough Edison bulbs, seemed to be the favorite haunt for tall, handsome boys on their lonesome. They all looked nice, and none of them had bottles of spit on their repurposed driftwood tables. The place was large enough that it would be awkward for her to pace aimlessly between the tables like an SAT examiner, but it was also small enough that she'd look stupid if she asked an employee for help. Besides, what could they say? It wasn't as though they…

Loretta sidled up to the barista, a college student who looked like a Mumford and Sons song brought to life, and leaned on the counter the way people did in movies when they were very casual and confident and definitely not so nervous that their insides felt like they could slide right out at the least disturbance, like if the sun came out from behind a cloud too quickly. "Did you make a drink for somebody named Arnold?"

"Today?" The barista asked as he made a show of fiddling with his big silver machine, pulling levers and pushing buttons, provoking it to hiss and whistle and leak like an over-the-hill New York construction worker when a pretty lady walks by.

"Oh, yeah, sorry," Loretta replied, because she had a habit of living life as though her motto was *Paeniteo Ergo Sum,* "I meant today."

"Probably." *Psssssh*, said the big silver machine.

"Um…I'm here to meet him, but I actually haven't met him before, so I was wondering if you c-"

HfweeeeeeeCLUNK. Psssshkerchunk.

"…could maybe po-"

"Marp!" the barista cried.

Shaken slightly, Loretta glanced down at the cup, which did indeed have the word 'Marp' scrawled on it. Recovering herself, she abandoned her preamble and dove in to the body of her appeal: "…could point Arnold out to me?"

The barista sighed and wiggled his meticulously curled mustache. "I would if I could, but I honestly don't put faces to these. I just call 'em out and do the next. When Tyler's working, that's him there with the neck tattoo," he indicated one of the cashiers with a tilt of his head, "he purposely puts down words that aren't real names just to mess me up. Unless Marp is a name, which, I don't know. But he sure doesn't write 'Arnold'. Lelsie!"

Loretta noted that, yes, this cup said 'Lelsie', so at least the barista was paying attention to *something*.

"Ok, thank you. Sorry."

Well, what was more embarrassing? Doing a lap around the café and potentially looking a bit silly, or standing here and raking her eyes around the room like a plainclothes cop? Without giving herself time to answer that question, Loretta waded into the pool of tall, handsome, and also nice boys clicking away at keyboards and scribbling away at moleskins. And just like a woman in a riddle, she emerged from the pool perfectly dry.

Okay, so *now* what was more embarrassing – the latter option in the first formulation, or texting Arnold and saying 'hey which lonely boy in La Reudugier are you?' Rachel had shown her a picture of Arnold! He'd looked so handsome and also nice (without reference, height was impossible to gauge)! It hadn't even occurred to her to commit the photo to memory, until she found herself here, in a room full of boys all auditioning for the same role.

Her phone buzzed. She pulled it out and saw a message from Arnold, courtesy of a platoon of brilliant little robots: 'hey did you just walk by me?'

Trying to hide her relief, she typed a reply ('yea that was probably me haha didn't see you though') and shot it up into outer space where it bounced off of a satellite, circled the Earth three times and came roaring back down into a tiny computer a few yards away from where it originated.

'hahaha' came the response, which wasn't especially helpful.

Loretta looked around the café. Nobody was looking up at her. All of them were looking at their phones. Perfect. 'where are you sitting again? Haha'

At long last: the bray of a chair leg scooting across hardwood. Arnold rose to his full height, and favored Loretta with a big, dopey grin. "Loretta?"

"Yeah!" she confirmed, a bit too enthusiastically. "Arnold?"

"Yes ma'am!" he reassured her, as though there were literally any chance that someone not-Arnold would have approached her here and asked her if she was named Loretta.

"Oh cool," Loretta said, just before throwing open the hatch to the subbasements of her mind and falling down the stairs of rumination. She had arrived at a flashpoint – hug, handshake or hee hee? Whatever course of action she chose would set the tone for the rest of this conversation, which could in turn chart a path for whatever future they may or may not have together. If she stepped forward and embraced him, tastefully and cautiously, as a grown man would embrace his best friend's adolescent daughter, might he misinterpret that? Not that Loretta even knew what would be meant by it. She wasn't a big hugger - more due to lack of opportunity than interest – but hugging was the thing people did on those commercials for online dating websites. So it was definitely a thing. But would Arnold know it was a thing? Had he seen the same commercials for online dating websites? Or would he think she was coming on to him, that she was loose, that he could pork her without a pigskin, or whatever euphemism Rachel was taking out on the town this week, use her for her body and go have a real relationship with a girl who was smarter and thinner and bustier and wealthier? Would Arnold think her a slut if she hugged him?

But, what if he knew all about commercials for online dating websites, and knew when a hug was just two folks squishing their sternums together, hips pulled back to well outside their respective blast radii? And what if she rushed forward, hand extended, like she was eager to close a business deal before the markets shuttered for the day? Might he think she was stiff and cold, an ice queen incapable of tenderness or feeling? Would his hand be stayed from the arch of her lower back as they walked down the street? Might he blanche from a romantic gesture, knowing that nothing blooms in the bosom of winter? Was there a chance he'd feel her limp, sweaty handshake and consider how little use he had for such a feeble grip?

Or would she do what she always did upon meeting someone new, which is to stand a safe distance away and go 'hee, hee' at regular intervals until they stopped staring at her?

Three options, each with pros and cons. Unfortunately, the entire deliberative process had a great big con, which was that she had no brilliant little robots to speed things along. She'd been standing here for a solid two seconds, which according to the laws of First Date Temporal Dilation, was actually one trillion years.

"Um," Arnold slipped through his melting smile, "would you like to sit down?"

"Yes, yes." It took everything Loretta had to keep from smacking herself on the forehead.

"Did you want something to drink? My treat," Arnold offered.

"Oh! Um…I think I'm ok," Loretta replied, even though she actually did want something to drink. Due to a reflexive refusal of any proffered refreshment (perhaps subconsciously believing that the offer was pro forma, and/or that acceptance would inconvenience the profferer), she spent most of her social life being thirsty and hungry. It was really annoying.

Arnold waved the offer away like a fart. "Sure, no worries. Do you mind if I'm sipping this while we talk?" He wrapped his calloused fingers around the cup before him.

"As long as it's not your own spit," some passing demon forced her mouth to say. No! Bad demon!

People don't talk about their spit on the first date!

Somehow, Arnold was not completely incensed by this. He lifted the cup and held it just in front of his mouth. "What if it's somebody else's?"

He was bantering! That was something Loretta had heard about, on a podcast or something. She'd never bantered, but best as she could tell it was the more mature equivalent of pulling on pigtails. "Then that's alright," she bantered back.

Arnold took a sip and wiggled his eyebrows around. It would probably have absolutely killed at a seven-year-old's birthday party.

"Whose spit is it?" Loretta bantered again.

"I was kidding. It *is* my spit."

"Oh," she continued to banter, "then that is not alright."

Arnold's face communicated that any given banter can only provide a certain amount of conversational propellant, and Loretta had tried to wring a bit too much from this banter. To extricate herself from the tailspin, she said "actually I think I will get something to drink. Not spit," she bantered one last time, "but coffee."

As Loretta rose to fetch herself a lovely cup of coffee, she finally decided that hugging was what she ought to have done upon first meeting Arnold.

The barista pronounced her name 'Lortorto', razzed her a bit about Arnold, and finally handed her a small latte. It was all so much white noise to her; she was focused on redemption. What could she say, upon retaking her seat, that would not only shrug off the dissonant overture so recently concluded, but set them on a more melodious path for the rest of the day? Boy, I'm always a bit loopy before I get my caffeine for the day. Gosh, I was just taken aback by how handsome you are. Gee, I spaced out a little, wondering how a just God could permit suffering.

So lost was she in her quest for exculpation, she walked right past Arnold again. Maybe? She scanned the café and saw a number of faces that all looked pretty much the same.

…which one was Arnold again? She'd just been talking to him! How could she have forgotten his face already? She'd found his smile to be so winning. And yet, all of these boys had winning smiles. At La Reudugier, everyone was a winner. Except Loretta.

She turned on her heel, wincing as a rogue wave of latte sloshed out through the sippyhole and scorched the lower knuckle of her thumb. Someday, when she and Arnold had been married long enough to have had a rough patch and gotten through it, she would tell this tale to their three children and they would all laugh. When Mommy first went out with Daddy, she kept fo-

Finally, she saw him. Chuckling to herself and finding her trusty self-deprecating smile right where she left it, she reached for the chair and turned on a dime because goddamnit it wasn't him.

Ah. Over there. *There* he was.

"Sorry," Arnold mumbled to his phone as Loretta

sat back down. "My fantasy team's not doing so hot." Inside Loretta's head, a choir sang hosannas to the predictability of jocks; Arnold had been staring at his phone, and so hadn't seen her stumbling, roundabout return.

"Not a problem," said the outside of Loretta's head. "*I'm* sorry, I came in a bit scatterbrained. Caffeine makes it all better."

"Yes it does," Arnold chuckled.

Loretta chuckled, sipped her drink, and despaired. This was small talk. Coffee is nice, isn't it? Yes it is, ha ha ha. Next they would be telling each other that they liked to laugh. There wasn't much Loretta hated more than small talk, s-

"Have you been here before?" Arnold asked.

No no no no no "No," Loretta replied.

"I have."

"It's a nice place."

"Yes," Arnold agreed, "it is. I'm pretty sure the name doesn't mean anything though. I looked it up online and couldn't find anything other than this place's Yelp." She could see, from the look in his eye, that Arnold felt the room deflating just as much as she.

Loretta, who had never been one to read a room properly, said "I bet it's just an excuse for hipsters to gargle their 'r's. I hate when people adopt accents for single words, you know?"

Arnold smiled and shrugged. "I guess it depends."

They sat and sipped their drinks. The caffeine did not make it all better.

Things got better when Loretta forgot to be self-conscious and asked Arnold what the most dangerous thing he'd ever done was. Not an especially probing question, but one that elicited a functionally engaging answer about free climbing in Colorado. He volleyed back the same question, which Loretta could only blushingly answer with a tale about being in the ocean when lightning struck a half-mile or so off the coast. This segued into more anecdotes, the exchange of ambitions and hopes and dreams, and finally a brief detour into the valley of the shadow of death. Arnold said he didn't want to know when he was going to expire, his preference being a death as swift as an on-coming train. Loretta, meanwhile, would much prefer a bit of forewarning, to get her affairs in order. That's what she said, anyway, even if she really meant to use her last days on Earth to settle old scores, and say the things she'd always wanted to say to people but never had the courage. She didn't say this to Arnold, though. She'd just remembered to be self-conscious.

Somehow, the scourge of small talk had burned itself out, giving an interesting conversation room to flourish. Loretta had seldom experienced such a natural progression. Unfortunately, it was cut short by another natural progression: the combination of her nerve-worried tummy and the caffeine.

"I'm actually gonna run to the restroom," she informed him as she rose to her feet. "Do you want anything while I'm up?"

"Nah, I'm all set. I'll just be here obsessing over my

made up football team."

Loretta chuckled and waddled to the restroom as quickly as she dared.

Gloriously divested of her breakfast, Loretta returned to La Reudugier proper. "Fuck me," she said aloud as she realized that, once again, she could not remember which of the generically attractive boys in the room was Arnold. They were all kind of tall, they were all looking at screens...*goddamnit*, she'd had a wonderful conversation with him for two hours! How was this possible? She summoned up his face from memory, and saw it as though reflected in a dirty puddle.

Taking yet another lap around the café, she examined the bone structure of each of the handsome boys. You could cut a wedding cake on his jawline, she remembered that much. But all of these fit fellas had sharply tapering jowls.

This was stupid. She was panicking for no reason. It was a fairly small café, and Arnold was somewhere inside of it. Taking her time, she took a preemptive victory lap, until she finally found him, yet again. Jesus. It was like combing the beach for a specific seashell; once you found it the differences were obvious enough. But from a distance, it was indistinguishable from the rest.

"All good?" he asked, which seemed like a silly question because if the answer was *no*, would he expect her to tell him?

Resisting the urge to say the sort of gross thing she'd commonly deploy on Rachel, she smiled and said "yes."

"So what were we talking about?"

"We were…" Loretta froze, halfway through a shuffling in her seat. What *had* they been talking about? It all seemed terribly interesting at the time, but here on the far side of the shithouse, she couldn't recall a single thing.

In her mind there was a door, and from behind the door there came a knocking. It was a thought, a strange and unexpected one, a thought that despite being popular, despite being athletic, despite being tall and handsome and also nice…Arnold was boring. Loretta hadn't yet opened the door, but she'd peeped through the keyhole, and rested her hand on the knob.

Feeling more and more hospitable by the moment, she ventured "I think we were talking about our ambitions."

"Oh," Arnold said, "right. I think I'd really love to be an airline pilot."

"Really? You fly?"

"No. Just seems like it'd be interesting. Like the guy from Iron Maiden."

"Oh. Are you gonna get a pilot license?"

"Probably not," he said. And then he said a lot more things. Over the next few minutes, Loretta opened that door in her mind, invited that thought into her mind, told it to put its feet up and make itself at home, made it hot chocolate, and made up the pullout bed.

"Nice but boring," she told Rachel that night.

Rachel nodded without taking her eyes from the

dance video on her laptop. "I could have told you that."

"Why didn't you?"

"Shhh." Rachel pointed to her laptop. "This is the best part. Just watch."

Loretta just watched, and agreed that the part in question was indeed the best one. When it was over, she reiterated her question.

"Because, if I'd told you he was boring, you might not have gone. I wanted to get you a date. It'd been a while, right?"

"Right. I appreciate that."

"I've dated a lot of assholes. Arnold's not one of them. He's just boring."

Loretta nodded. This was all true.

Rachel's eyes went wide. "Oooh, have you seen Dana Wilson? She's *so good*." She clicked on the video, which they watched. It was indeed *so good*, and by the end of it, Loretta had already forgotten about Arnold, yet again.

The next day, Arnold called her to remind her that he existed. He said he'd had a great time, and would love to hang out again. In a moment she would always consider to be a turning point in her relationship with herself, Loretta, the socially irrelevant dork, told the popular, handsome and also nice boy that she had also enjoyed their coffee date, and she'd absolutely love to continue hanging out with him, but only as friends. She just wasn't looking for anything right now. None of this was a lie, but it was a glossy version of the truth. Fortunately, Arnold concurred.

This did not augur an epochal shift in Loretta's life. She and Arnold hung out a few more times, Arnold going so far as to invite her to a party once. It had been a rather bro-y affair, but had been enjoyable nonetheless. Over time, they developed an honest (if not particularly robust) friendship. At the end of that year, Arnold graduated and went to college out of state. The brilliant little robots were busy with their correspondence for a few months, but gradually had less and less business to conduct on Loretta and Arnold's behalf.

For the rest of her high school career, Loretta teetered right on the precipice of both popularity and unpopularity, but never overbalanced in either direction. This proved a stroke of luck; by the time she was flipping the tassel to the left side of her stupid square hat, she could consider herself on speaking terms with just about everybody in the school. To say she acquired any degree of comfort or facility with socialization would be to overshoot the mark. What she gained was the self-confidence to take her manifold embarrassments in stride.

Years later, after she and her husband and been married for long enough to have had a rough patch and gotten through it, she recalled the day unmemorable little Loretta had told the boring popular kid that she wasn't interested in dating him. She didn't share this with anyone – there was no question that, like any cherished keepsake, it would only reveal its significance to her – but it always made her laugh.

which mongolian warlord do you want on your team in
charades

can-guess khan

what did jesus say at the pool party

come on in, the water's wine

who was the most well connected president in american
history

abraham linkedin

GOOSIN' BRUISER

Let's say you want a guy whacked. You know – rubbed out. In the way his girlfriend *don't* do. Well. Unless she does. Some guy's girls do. Sobotka, up in New York? Awfully generous, when it came to the dames. One of 'em gets jealous. Next thing I hear, the poor son of a bitch is takin' up both sides of the bed. Lady cut him straight in half, like she took the crack in his ass for a suggestion. Not often you see a made guy go out like a wishbone. Coulda buried him in a pair of baguette sleeves. Lotta laughs at his funeral. Closed casket, very respectful.

That's the kinda amateur hour rubbin' out I was talkin' about, just a second ago. If it ain't gotta be clean or quiet, but it's gotta be *done*, then the only reason it ain't done yet is on accounta you're draggin' ass to the boardwalk. Put it this way; I'd give you fifty bucks outta my pocket if you could find the one lummock down there who *wouldn't* do it.

But that's for your basic mess job. Let's say you want somebody *taken care of*. Also not the way girlfriends do, but let's not talk about Sobotka again. Sometimes two slugs to the gut sends the wrong message. Maybe you need a guy gone, like *really* gone. Like the kinda gone gets gumshoes scratching themselves bald. Or maybe it's gotta look like a case of the natural causes. Or the kind of accident ain't gettin' called out by a tricky dick.

You go back down the boardwalk, try to find somebody can promise you that and deliver. I'll put my fifty back on the table. Take your time. Don't worry, I'll keep flappin' the dust off. I want it to be nice, for when I put it back in my pocket.

There's only one guy in Atlantic City can make that promise and deliver. Ain't a fuckin' coincidence. You ask anybody who should I talk to about my problem, and they'll tell you: you want Samuzzo D'Amato.

Some people figure that's a funny name, 'til I pop 'em on the nose.

You laughin'?

Didn't think so.

So anyway, it's four in the morning, and I'm staring at my toaster. Ain't everybody can afford a toaster. I can. It's only right, the guy at the top of his field sets his own price. I set it high. Lets me buy nice things. Like a toaster.

It's a nice toaster. I wouldn't buy a toaster wasn't nice. It's all silver and shiny. I can see myself in it. A fat rectangle me. It's funny. I laugh, and so does the toaster.

So I pop the toaster on my nose. It throws two

pieces of bread at me and clicks real loud. I jump. Anybody would.

I shake my head at the toaster and toss the toast onto the toast pile. I pull two more pieces of bread off the bread pile, stuff 'em down those stupid toaster holes, and lean on the lever.

Then I just wait. Before long this asshole breadbox is gonna screw up some courage and throw more bread at me. And it's gonna click real loud. I think it's the click gets me.

I just gotta see it happen. Gotta keep my eyes open. Gotta not flinch.

See, here's the thing. I'm *the* guy you go to, you need a problem taken care of. Remember I was just tellin' you about that? I'll work for anybody. I got no formal connections. I follow the money. People respect that. And if they don't, I go ring their doorbell. They open the door, I lean in. They gotta take a step back and look up. Everybody respects *that*.

I'm a bruiser, is what I'm saying. A tough. I'm *the* tough in town. But I also got this problem. I goose easy. Somebody slams a door too loud, I jump. Car horn honks while I'm walkin' down the street, I jump. One time I'm sittin' on this guy with bad luck and a deep bathtub. Few minutes later I climb out, start dryin' things up. I bend over to grab a towel, and I fart. Toughs fart too.

But I also jumped. Toughs don't jump. Lucky me, the guy in the tub was lookin' at somethin' else.

I know there's rumors. Nobody's ever come and

tried them out to my face, but I hear 'em. Oh, D'Amato'll dance if you catch him right. Yeah, Sammy's feet don't get along with the floor. Ha, he's the toughest guy in the room, long as there ain't no Jack-in-the-Box around.

What's my least favorite about all that is, somebody gets it into their head to sneak up and try one of those out behind my back, I might go and prove 'em right.

Is that gonna be curtains for Samuzzo D'Amato? Is somebody gonna send the second-best tough in town to punch my card? I ain't worried. Really, worst that'll happen is people stop comin' to me. Go to the second-best. So maybe I gotta beat them there. And to the third and fourth best. Maybe they keep comin' to me anyway, if all of a sudden only the fifth-best is answerin' his phone.

But still. They'll laugh. I can pop a few guys, but I can't pop 'em all. Wherever I go, they'll be slammin' doors and honkin' horns. Look at Sammy dance. They'll probably give me a nickname. Made it this long without one. I don't want a damn nickname.

So I gotta not jump. Gotta teach myself. Don't goose.

The toaster throws bread at me. And that fuckin' click. Two more for the toast pile, two more from the bread.

I got twenty hours 'til the meet. I'm gonna need more bread.

GOOSIN' BRUISER

Whole ride out, Longie keeps tellin' me shit that ain't got nothin' to do with me. But what else is new. I could brain him and run his rackets, and nobody'd be the wiser. That's how much he tells me about it. I don't on accounta I'm just a hell of a guy.

Credit where it's due, the dope's got hustle. He was a bootlegger when we first got together. Working for Luciano. He bought his booze in Canada, shipped it down on boats and trucks. Got it to Rum Row on speedboats, painted black. Real excitin' stuff. Meanwhile up in Philly, Waxy Gordon's boys figure out you can still make grain alcohol, if you got the right credentials. So they have a parlay, next thing you know Longie's cuttin' Luciano's illegal booze with Gordon's legal booze. Everybody profits.

See where I fit in there? Neither the fuck do I.

But every time we're headin' for a pick up, or makin' a drop, he starts givin' me all the context. Context, that's what he says. So I says, I don't need context to knock two heads together. He always liked that. Just not as much as *context*.

Somebody in Washington stamped somethin', and now we don't need bootleggers no more. That was fine by Longie. He'd moved on. Last year Schultz gets whacked at the chophouse, now everybody's callin' Longie our very own Capone. I'm workin' with him all the while. Not *for* him. I follow the money, like I said. Just so happens Longie's got the most of it.

Sometimes as he's handin' me my cut he says gee Sammy, you must feel pretty lucky. So I says yeah, you too. He smiles, only I don't figure he likes that one so much.

Anyways, tonight we're goin' to a meet about labor unions, if you can believe it. Even more complicated than the booze. And Longie's tellin' me all about it. Most nights I'm happy to let him run it out. I don't know if he don't get out much or he don't like the sound of my voice or what. Ain't for me to know. I just gotta listen. Like, really listen. Sometimes he accidentally asks me what do I think about anything. I gotta be able to answer. It's part of the job, way I see it.

I can't focus tonight though. I'm thinkin' about toasters.

Two days ago, soon as Longie tells me about this meet, Nutelli gives me a tip. That's one of Longie's right hand men. Probably got a stupid title, like lieutenant or colonel or some shit. Why Longie wants me on these meets when he's got a lunk like Nutelli, I'll never know. But he pays me, so I don't need to.

Anyway, Nutelli gives me a tip. I figure he heard some of those rumors about me. I figure he was too smart to laugh at them.

Gotta admit, the guy had balls even talkin' to me about it.

Nutelli says, listen, I'm just givin' you notice, one professional to another. There's gonna be a wiry little guy at the meet. Part of the union crew. Like a little dog thinks he's big, this guy. He likes to jump at you. Make like he's comin' for ya. To test people. See if they goose.

I just look at him for a minute. Tryin' to figure out is he laughin' at me or not. I decide he ain't, so I say whaddya mean.

Nutelli repeats himself.

So I says thanks and do me a favor and shut up about it.

He gets it. Good guy, that guy.

First thing I do is go out and buy a toaster.

After two nights and I don't know how many breads, I'm better. I don't goose as big. I still goose though. A little bit.

Maybe too much.

So I'm thinkin' about toasters, all the while Longie's going on and on. Eventually he says SAMMY, you listenin'?

I jump when he says Sammy. Not a lot. Just a little bit.

So I says ah, shit.

Longie says what's shit? You been listenin' to me?

Now, I ain't scared of Longie the way a lot of other folks are. I like the guy. And not just on accounta he pays me. So I ain't lookin' to hurt his feelings by saying funny you should ask, I ain't listened to a good goddamn word you said because it ain't got nothin' to do with me.

So I play dumb. Never fails, with these guys. You can get away with anything, you just make 'em feel halfway smart.

I says I'm tryin', boss – they like that too, callin' em boss – only I ain't sure how can I wrap my head around this union stuff.

So he shrugs and gets this little smile on his face. And he says, that's alright, it's pretty tough to keep straight, you ain't got a razor sharp mind.

So I says, that's you alright. Razor sharp mind.

He says, you blowin' smoke up my ass?

So I says, you paid me yet?

He likes that one even more than context, I guess. Rest of the ride is real quiet.

I ain't one of those guys likes knockin' heads. You want a psycho, go back to the boardwalk. I do it on accounta I'm good at it. If it were my sayso, every meet would be civil as buyin' baseball cards. No reason for them to go otherwise. Then again, it's a good thing some of 'em do. I got no other skills.

Soon as Longie says we're here, I get an idea it's gonna be one of them civil nights. Nothin' kickin' off. And here's me, upset about it. Normally I'd be happy. But normally I ain't got a wiry little guy wantin' to goose me.

It's a picturehouse. Big white marquee says The General Died At Dawn, like I'm supposed to give a shit.

Longie, Nutelli and me, we meet the union guys in the lobby. There's three of them, and the guy in front says he's called Wilkerson. He calls the lobby a *foyer*. Pronounces it like he's got somethin' against the letter 'r'. I ain't worried about him.

Over his shoulders are a big son of a bitch and a

wiry little guy. Real slow, I nod to the big son of a bitch. The big son of a bitch nods back, real slow. This guy gets it. I ain't worried about him neither.

It's Tommy Toothpick over there I got my eye on. Whole time Longie and Wilkerson are schmoozin', Toothpick's got my full attention. He's bouncin' from toe to toe, hair floppin' around like it can't get comfortable. Before too long he sees me starin' and gives it right back. That's when he leans on the lever. Gets real still.

I got his number.

Here's the hard part. When's he gonna pop? He's gonna wait 'til I'm close, that's for sure.

What's the move? Do I keep my distance? I can look mean all night, standin' here. Harder to look mean when you're backpedaling from a guy small enough the doctor's still givin' him lollipops. So it ain't a matter of 'if'. Meet breaks, he's gonna come walkin' up to me like we're old chums. Then he'll try it. Maybe I beat him to it. Jump at *him*. See who gooses.

That's the move. I'm happy with that. So I settle in to wait for the meet to break…

Longie don't sound right. He's talkin' slow, sayin' um a lot. Longie ain't the kinda guy says um a lot. He works real hard to use pretty words. You always know they're comin' when the vein on his forehead starts pumpin'.

I turn to look at what's got his tongue. Only I think about that big son of a bitch over there. So I turn slow.

I guess Toothpick was bankin' on a faster turn. I

catch him dartin' his eyes to Nutelli. Then back to me.

Ah, shit.

Now I get why Longie brings me out to his business meetings. When I'm plyin' my trade I do things clean, like I said earlier. But sometimes clean means messy, long as the mess don't trail to your front door.

This is gonna be one of those.

I grab Longie by the shoulder. He says hey what's the b-, then I throw him across the room, flat, so he slides like Gehrig makin' for the platter.

That's got *me* movin' just like I want. I swing right through the space Longie used to be takin' up, headin' straight for Nutelli.

He's already reachin' for his gun.

I don't much like guns myself. Or knives. Time you spend learnin' how to use a gun or a knife right is time you don't spend on your body. Then somebody slaps your hardware outta your hand, whaddya got then? Whereas, I got big heavy arms. You pull 'em outta their sockets, I can still swing 'em at you from the torso.

I really like it when *other* people use guns and knives.

I spin out in front of him, straight on. So the angle's right. Still movin', I use one hand to snatch his bean shooter. The other one bunches into a fist. And since my arm ain't outta it's socket, there's a lotta muscle drivin' it into Nutelli's face, one, two, three times. Somethin' snaps and he falls asleep.

That's one.

I keep whirlin' around and the big son of a bitch is chargin' me. Turns out slow ain't a hobby for him. It's a goddamned lifestyle. Well, not for long.

He comes shamblin' with his arms out. Stick some bolts in his neck and he's ready for Halloween. You get the picture. Here's a problem. I gotta let him get his hands on me. Only way to get the angle right. But corner of my eye, I see Wilkerson's fishin' a piece outta his sock. Toothpick's got a knife and he's makin' a play for Longie.

Toothpick's gonna fuck this up.

Finally, the big son of a bitch makes it to me. He clamps his hands onto my shoulders. I jam the gun up into bottom of his jaw and pull the trigger. The top of his head blows off. Like he had a bright idea for once and his brain couldn't handle it.

That's two.

I push the big son of a bitch's body straight back. As he falls, I get a clean shot at Wilkerson. I plug him in the gut, so he don't die. Longie's gonna wanna chat.

Talkin' of Longie, Toothpick's practically on top of him.

So I says hey shithead.

And the shithead spins around and takes a shot at me.

It misses. But I hear a *ping* behind me. Left a fuckin' hole.

So I says fuck! Real loud. I guess the wiry little guy took that as my dyin' breath, on accounta he turns back to chase Longie, who finally got up off his ass. Boss finally figured there were comfier spots to lay down.

I take off runnin'. I ain't gonna catch him though.

That little guy can move. I'm too big to move like that.

I got a gun. But I don't wanna shoot him in the back. I'm tryin' to make a, whaddya call it, a scene. Wilkerson might call it a *tableau*. Yeah, I know that word. Ain't as dumb as I look.

Point is, I gotta wrap this up in a bow. Luciano's got some cops in his pocket. Longie calls Luciano, Luciano calls his boys in blue. Long as there's somethin' pretty to write, they can make a case go away. Long investigation's somethin' else.

I had it all set up. Angles were just right. Some guys makin' a deal that went four bodies south. All I had to do was catch Toothpick right in the neck with a bullet. Simple.

Course he goes and blows it.

I run outside. Nobody's out tonight, which is nice.

It's a quiet part of town. Well lit, too. Those things ain't so nice.

Longie and Toothpick are makin' a hell of a racket. They're clompin' down the center of the street, hootin' and hollerin'.

I gotta think this reflects on me. I got played. Nutelli tells me keep an eye on the wiry little guy. 'Cause he heard those fuckin' rumors. So what do I do but keep an eye. I'm so focused on Toothpick, I tune out the double-cross.

If only I didn't goose so easy.

Ah, well.

I run back inside. Grab the car key outta Nutelli's pocket. Wilkerson's still screamin', clutchin' his belly like that'll help.

I says to him, quit screamin', you'll live longer. Who knows if that's true. But it stops him screamin'.

I go back out. Start up the car.

I look up as I'm guidin' it out into the street. Hell if Longie still ain't givin' Toothpick a workout. Gotta laugh at that. Night's goin' to shit, but that's pretty funny.

If Toothpick knew he had a Packard on his ass, he never let on. Never tried to turn around. Last thing I see of him as he's slidin' under the front bumper was the back of his head, hair floppin' every which way like it's tryin' to save itself.

He went under the first tire like normal. When he went under the second, I guess his ribs caved or somethin' on accounta the car dipped pretty hard before he was out from under.

The car had good breaks. Lucky for Longie.

I says to him, hey Longie!

He just keeps runnin' for another couple of yards.

So I call his name again.

He stops and turns around. I never seen him so white.

All he says is what the hell, Sammy. I liked that car.

So I says I woulda thought you'd like it more than ever now.

He just throws his hands up.

So I says you wanna talk to Wilkerson or what?

I make him walk back to the picturehouse. I gotta get rid of the car. First I double check the wiry little guy's dead. He ain't quite, so I give him a face massage. Now he is. Hit and run. Real tragic.

Then I remember that other hole in the picture-house, the one in a place don't make any sense for my *tableau*. I gotta get rid of the car, then I gotta do fuckin' renovations. I'll tell ya, if it ain't one thing, it's always another.

Couple hours later I walk back in and Longie says hey Sammy, break this guy's knees.

So I go step on Wilkerson's knees. Then I say to Longie what, this guy not talkin'?

And he says oh he's talkin' alright, he's spillin' his guts. Then he laughs and points to Wilkerson's tummy leakin' all over the *foyer* carpet.

I laugh on accounta I ain't been paid yet.

And he tells me the whole fuckin' story. Basic power play. Wilkerson was workin' for Capone – the real Chicago Capone, not Atlantic City's Capone – but figured he could do better on his own. He bounces out to Jersey, gets knocked around the casino front. Wants to see how can he get a piece of anything, everybody says you gotta see Atlantic City's Capone. That'd be Longie. Well, Wilkerson wasn't too pleased about that. Figures he'll just off the boss. Not the brightest.

I'm not really listenin'. I'm puttin' the finishing touches on my *tableau*. Bustin' knuckles, smearin' blood, thinkin' about how I got fuckin' played.

After Longie hears everything he wants to, he says to me how should we do it.

So I says let him bleed out.

He says what if he doesn't and he's alive when the cops show up.

I says fair enough. So I put my hand over Wilkerson's face for a few minutes.

I wipe my fingertip prints off Nutelli's gun with my sleeve. Every once in a while they get somebody on those. You believe that shit? Better safe than sorry, I say.

Then I put the gun back in Nutelli's hand.

Anybody asks, we were never there.

We're walkin' back towards Longie's place, thinkin'. It's still mostly night, but day's startin' to get some funny ideas behind the trees. Finally I says to Longie what I gotta say sooner or later. If I wanna keep callin' myself a professional. I says to him I'm real sorry about that boss, I shoulda seen that comin'.

He says to me nevermind that. I should have too.

So I says that's awful nice to say, but that's not your job. It's mine.

He says no, really. I shoulda known something was up. I mean, I know all the guys in the union here, but I'd never seen that Wilkerson character in my life.

So I says what the hell do you mean, we go to a meeting with a guy you ain't never seen and you don't tip me?

He says how was I supposed to do that?

So I says gimme an elbow or something. Jesus.

We're both real quiet for a while. Then he says to me

I really liked that car.

He didn't say nothin' about Nutelli, so I didn't bring it up.

When we get back he pays me in small bills.

By the time I get home it's tomorrow. I dump my bags out on the table and wash my hands.

I fold my arms and size it up. My project for the day. Six loaves of bread. The pre-sliced kind. I don't buy bread ain't been pre-sliced.

I open 'em all up. Make a brand new bread pile. Put two pre-sliced slices in the toaster holes. Lean on the lever.

Then I just wait.

why do people put amphibians on the ground to
improve their reflexes

it keeps them on their toads

what did the man say to the swamp he wanted to own

i'm gonna bayou

what is a scientist's most trusted form of romantic
assignation

a double-blind date

HAZARDS

HAZARDS

She pulled in front of the fire hydrant, put on her hazards, and threw the car into park. That was something.

And he didn't get out immediately. That was something.

They just sat, listening to the song on the radio and the CLICK click CLICK click CLICKing of the hazards disagreeing about the speed at which the world should run. It was an unpleasant little cacophony, and still, he didn't get out. That was something.

The evening had been full of 'something's, weighty intimations of concepts she couldn't bring herself to express. At least, she thought so. She *hoped* so. Hints of a romantic sort are best dropped delicately, like the pedal of a rose lilting gently to the ground.

(Or maybe don't compare your love life to a dying flower, huh?)

But that sort of social finesse had never been her strong suit; she tended to drop those hints with all the subtlety of a goat falling off a cliff. Which was why, as of late, she'd taken to forgoing the drop entirely. She was a twenty-first century woman, but perhaps there was something to be said for letting the guy make the first move. Perhaps that would save her the familiar humiliations of a bleating descent and a halting *splat*.

Assuming this guy was going to make the first move. Assuming he *wanted* to make the first move. Assuming that was a move he had any intention of making, first or otherwise.

But.

She had thrown the car into park and he hadn't gotten out immediately. That was something.

But.

On the ride home, he'd cranked the AC without asking, when she'd already mentioned she was cold earlier in the evening. That was something *else*.

But.

He'd offered her his jacket when she had mentioned she was cold. *That* was something.

But. But. But. She could keep going on forever, and get no closer to sussing out what he felt. Her feelings were abundantly clear to her. Well, sort of. Maybe not. But she had a lot of feelings, and that was a cast-iron certainty. Basically. For the most part.

Either way, she was getting fed up with waiting. They were both intelligent, mature individuals. It'd be the easiest thing in the world, to sit down over a lovely cup of coffee and have an intelligent, mature conversation about their feelings. It'd be the easiest thing in the world to figure it out from there, once all the intelligent, mature cards were on the table.

But.

It's also the easiest thing in the world for a goat to fall off a cliff, isn't it? Gravity does all the work; the only hard part is the landing. The easiest things in the world are usually the ones from which you can't come back.

So she sat with him in the car, some song or other playing quietly from a neighboring galaxy, hazards CLICK click CLICK click CLICKing out their own relentless rhythm, marking the inexorable passage of time. And for an eternity and a half they were silent, listening to the curious discord of the song and the hazards, each banging out their own beats, heedless of the other.

The two of them sat in the car until, for just a second or two, the dueling rhythms converged. For just a second or two, there was perfect concord, and everything made sense. And after a second or two, the tempos reclaimed their independence and fell back out of step.

But.

In that second or two, he had looked at her, and she had looked at him. And if there wasn't *perfect* concord, and if not *everything* made sense...well, they could figure it out.

That was something.

what do you call it when someone dissects a puppy to
determine the cause of death

an awwwtopsy

what do you call someone who trades sex for spaghetti

a pastatute

which species of primate lawyer takes all of their cases
for free

pro bonobos

TAKERS

TAKERS

Idiots. He could spot a taker from a block and a half away. The flat twinkle in the eye, the slight quickening of the step. All the same.

He didn't have to move a muscle. Just stand, smile, and let them come to him.

This latest taker was slimmer than his usual quarry. If he felt the slightest misgiving, it was quickly extinguished. The yokel had an ugly wife – maybe a sister, it wouldn't surprise him – and two fat kids. He was just like the others, even if he didn't look like it at first.

Besides, Gareth was casting a wide net. Didn't those guys who farmed tuna wind up with a few dolphins every now and then? A small price to pay.

The yokel trailed his awful brood right up to Gareth. Approachable Gareth, standing and smiling.

With practiced amiability, Gareth leaned forward and extended the tray. Just the slightest bit. Just enough to seal the deal. It was almost funny, how easily people would yield to just a hint of solicitation.

When it became *actually* funny was when they took

the cookie.

"Free samples?" The yokel gurgled.

Gareth smiled as hard as he could. "Yes, sir!"

And that was all it took. The yokel palmed a cookie off Gareth's tray and shoveled it straight into his mouth, without even engaging his fingers. That approach always sickened and elated Gareth in equal measure.

"Would your family like one?" Gareth asked.

"No thank you," the sisterwife replied. "I'm trying to watch my figure."

Gareth chuckled at that. He trusted she was too dumb to understand why. "And what about these," the word caught in his throat, "adorable little kiddos?"

The gremlins bounced and bubbled like farts in a tub. "Ooooh mommy daddy can we can we can we?!?" They sounded exactly like alarm clocks.

Daddy looked to Mommy, who mooned at her spawn.

To, ha, *sweeten* the deal, Gareth said "these actually have seventy percent less sugar than any other cookie on the market." That was almost certainly not true. But what were they gonna do, take it to a lab?

If they did, they'd find a lot more to fuss about than sugar.

Mommy melted like the chocolate bars she undoubtedly had stuffed into her pockets. "Alright. You can each have *half* a cookie."

The children cheered. Gareth knelt down, bringing the tray to their level. He was all too happy to. "And how old are *you* two?" he asked as the bigger of the two palmed a cookie, just like Daddy.

"I'm six," the little shitsmear announced like it was something to be proud of, "and she's four." He broke the cookie in half and handed the smaller piece to his sister. Oh yes, this was a born taker.

Six and four. Gareth tried to guess height and weight. If his math was right, a half a dose each would still do the job. So he could let a bit of honesty seep into his smile.

"Six and four! Do you take good care of your sister?"

The kid nodded. Unlike Daddy, he used two hands to nibble on his cookie. Half of it was winding up on the sidewalk.

Gareth frowned and stood back up. "So what do you think of the cookies?"

"Real nice," the yokel boomed. His eyes were locked on the tray.

As if he needed a second. One was more than enough to get the job done. Gently as he'd leaned in, Gareth shifted his weight away from the family. The nuclear *waste* family. Ooh, that was good. He made a mental note of that.

"You folks have a great day now," Gareth smiled.

That disappointment splattered on the yokel's mug was probably the closest he'd ever get to being handsome. "You too," was all he said. And then he shuffled off into the punishing mid-day heat.

Once the heifers – yes, even if they weren't the

average taker, they could be honorarily inducted into their ranks – were out of earshot, Gareth allowed himself to really laugh. This was the best part. Watching them walk away, oblivious.

It never failed to astonish him. Nobody ever asked him who he worked for, or why he was standing in front of (he turned around) a law office and a boutique hat store, with a tray of unmarked cookies. Every once in a while somebody would ask him what was in them, more often than not because they had a food allergy. He wasn't even wearing an apron, or a hat, or *anything* to link him to a real establishment. He used to have a T-shirt onto which he'd silkscreened a fake bakery logo, but one day he forgot it and got just as many takers as any other day. Now it was like a game for him. How disreputable a front could he present, and still get takers?

So far, he'd never lost.

Here's what the future had in store for that inbred hick family. For a few days, they'll be fine. Then they'll get a tummyache. No worries, everybody gets those. They'll drain some Pepto and be on their way. Then they'll feel feverish. Chills, sweats, overwhelming fatigue. An agonizing dryness of the throat comes next. It'll burn to drink water, and any food they try to ingest will come back up, along with a half a cup of blood. If they aren't already bedridden by then, they'll be laid out by crippling vertigo. After that, they'll get a really bad rash. Small onions compared to the rest, but Gareth had worked hard on the compound to get that delayed release dermatological assault. Insult to injury, that sort of thing.

Then, and only then, does the poison start attacking the central nervous system. Muscle spasms, violent expectorations from every orifice, a shutdown of the digestive system. They languish like that for as long as it takes for them to starve. And Mommy will just have to watch, over days and days, as Daddy and her two little darlings gasped their last.

That'll teach 'em. Idiots.

He got a whole gaggle of tourists, most takers he'd ever hooked at once. Just four cookies left on the tray. But that was alright; it was tending towards sunset. He'd be heading home himself soon. He might even have time to synthesize more of his Special Sauce before he put on his stupid orange vest and went to work. The work that paid the bills, anyway

"Oooh," cooed some idiot woman over his shoulder, "do I see free cookies?"

Gareth never had to dig too deep to fetch that first grin for a new taker. He turned, proffering the tray in one balletic motion. "Yes, ma'am!"

The woman was a classic taker; fat, draped in a floral mumu, a fanny pack vanishing into her folds. She extended her hand halfway to the tray, making a little claw with her thumb and forefinger. "May I?"

"By all means."

The woman plucked a cookie from the tray as though she sensed its power. Just as delicately, she took a nibble. Not enough to do anybody any good.

She swirled the crumbs around her mouth like wine. "Hm," she pondered. "What's in this?"

Gareth caught his brow sliding towards his nose. "Are you concerned about a food allergy?"

"No, I'm just trying to place the taste."

"Oh, now, did you get *any* taste from such a small bite?"

"I did, and I'm trying to place it." Her nose was curled slightly.

Absurdly, Gareth's most overwhelming emotion was offense. How *dare* she curl her nose at his baking! "They're chocolate chip cookies."

"What bakery are they from?"

"I *made* them," Gareth snapped.

The woman blinked hard. "I'm sorry if I offended you. I'm an amateur baker. I'm trying to work on my palate."

Gareth had plenty of toothy digs for that level of pretention, but he recognized détente when he saw it. Nobody was gonna eat a cookie if they were agitated. "That's quite alright. I hope I didn't come off as overly aggressive. I'm just…trying a new recipe, is all."

Good will and fellowship christened her face once again. Gareth wanted to smash it. "So where's your bakery?" she asked.

For a moment, Gareth blanked on the name of his fictional establishment. Then it came to him. "Oh! It's called Leslie's. That's my boss' name, Leslie. It's his bakery. It's in, um, SoHo."

The woman seemed to be suppressing a laugh. Bitch. "Well, yes, that makes sense. Seeing as we're in SoHo. I figured he wouldn't send you here from, like, Queens."

Gareth ground his teeth. It was a testament to his superior genetics, that his chompers withstood his constant abuse without going all jagged. "I like to keep my cookie recipe close to the vest, you understand. But it's really just a, um, superior chocolate chip cookie."

"Hm," said the woman. She flipped the cookie around to investigate every side, like she was looking for the expiration date. "I thought I tasted almond. And then something fruitier, like...citrus, almost."

For just a split second, Gareth consider running. His compound was absolutely tasteless. Or so he'd assumed – he'd obviously never tasted it. Were his cookies actually bad? Had the takers just been humoring him this whole time? Impossible. No way that many of them had even a glancing familiarity with good manners. But he'd given them something free; maybe they felt bad...

"Is it not good?" Gareth detected an unbecoming whine in his voice.

The woman was still staring at the cookie. Finally she looked back up to Gareth. "Maybe it's just not for me." She tossed the cookie into a nearby garbage can.

She *tossed* the *cookie* in the *garbage*.

"Woah woah woah woah," Gareth huffed. "Hang on a second. You barely had a single bite. You couldn't even taste anything!"

She shrugged. "I'm just being honest. I'm not saying

it was bad, I don't believe in discouraging anybody from following their passions. I'm just giving you my honest opinion, so you can, I don't know, have it. Maybe try tweaking the recipe?"

"Tweaking the…" Gareth sputtered for a few seconds. "Lady, people love my cookies."

"I'm happy to hear that, sweetie," she mooed with unctuous sincerity. "So I'm gonna be the lone v-"

"Try another bite. A great big bite, see what you think."

"Why's it matter what one lady thinks of your cookies? Most people like them, why've I gotta like them too?"

"It's not about *liking* it, it's about whether or not you actually *ate* any!"

"Mister, stop shouting."

"I'm not shouting!" he shouted.

The woman took a deep breath. Gareth felt like she was doing it on his behalf. She was gonna eat a fucking cookie if he had to shove it down her fat, stupid throat. "I'm not trying to hurt your feelings. I'm just saying, I know baking's personal, and a lot of people won't give you honest opinions, because they don't wanna hurt your feelings. So I'm gi-"

"Did I ask for your opinion?"

"Nope," she shrugged. "I guess not. Sorry to bother you. Thanks for the cookie."

"That you didn't fucking eat."

That cow, that fucking bitch, she just shook her head at him and waddled back to the buffet, or wherever the fuck she was going.

The cookies on the tray were rattling. Gareth's arm was shaking. As were his knees. How dare she. How *dare* she. How dare she?!

A few people in his immediate vicinity were staring at him. They probably heard him swear. Alright, so he would have to ditch this corner earlier than expected.

He hung his head. The tectonic scraping in his jaw struck him like a tuning fork. He was thrumming. How dare she.

Naturally, his eye went to the cookies.

He stared at them for quite a while.

He couldn't. It would be idiotic.

But would a nibble hurt him? She'd gotten a taste from the tiniest little sample.

He needed to know.

Maybe a little crumb would make him sick for a day or two. That was worth it in the name of greater understanding, wasn't it?

He picked up a cookie.

Maybe he could just lick it.

He chuckled and put it back down.

It didn't matter what they tasted like. He baked them to cull the herd, to shuffle the takers of the world off to the great larder in the sky. It was stupid to worry about whether or not one of those takers did or didn't like his cookie. What did he care?

He palmed a cookie off his tray and lifted it to his mouth.

Tentatively, he caressed it with his tongue.

All he could taste was the cookie itself. The…what would you call it, the body? None of the notes.

He pulled his lips back and brought his markedly jagged teeth down on the tiniest portion of the cookie.

There was a definite citrus note to it. It was pretty overpowering. He couldn't really tell how it did or didn't, uh, pair with the rest of the, the body.

He took another little nibble. The tiniest nibble.

No almonds, just citrus and chocolate. It wasn't bad, really. What had that lady been on about, scrunching her nose like that? The citrus note was really more of an *orange* note. The orange note and the chocolate note blended, activating taste buds all up and down the tongue. That's how you knew it was a rich, complex cookie.

He took another itty bitty bite. One last one. Yes, there was some almond notes. But it was a beautiful blend with the other notes! The citrus was a little bit overpowering, sure. And there was now a kind of fishy note. Who knew how that one got there.

Alright, this was the last bite. He made it slightly bigger. Not too big, on the order of seven crumbs instead of three. There were all the notes at once. The seafood note was stronger now. It wasn't great. Good heavens, how had so many of the takers told him, to his face, that the cookies were great? Why had nobody been honest with him?

Gareth sighed and dumped the remaining two and a half cookies into the garbage can. He'd need to go home and work on the recipe. Perhaps a reevaluation of his synthesization techniques was also in order. Ugh. This was a project that would take several days. He was hoping to bang another batch out before work, then hit the streets with them tomorrow. But he couldn't be slinging a subpar cookie, could he? The idiots wouldn't care, but he would, damnit. He would.

Tail between his legs, Gareth drifted home.

For a few days, he was fine.

what tummy ailment afflicts people highly devoted to jewish orthodoxy

hasid reflux

why might you turn down a buy-one-get-one-free offer at an italian bakery

their goodies are so sweet, you cannoli eat one

what kinds of cookies do yoghis love most

chakra-t chip

HAS ANYBODY SEEN BURTON'S SHOES?

HAS ANYBODY SEEN BURTON'S SHOES?

The floor in the bathroom was wet, which wasn't what Burton Turnbo had expected of first class. It was also the same sort of bathroom as was tucked in the very back of the 777, on the other side of that gossamer blue curtain. He hadn't necessarily envisioned a *larger* bathroom up here, just maybe…nicer. Certainly not with a wet floor, though in fairness that was probably not part of the design.

Also in fairness, it was probably not the sort of thing he'd have noticed if he'd been wearing his shoes.

Burton Turnbo had lived forty-seven years of comfortable middle class life, and so viewed air travel with the casual utilitarianism of the have-somes. Flying was for getting from one place to another as quickly as possible, nothing more. Why spend nearly half again what you'd spend on a coach ticket to be slightly more comfortable for a few hours?

Besides, he often thought with a bit too much self-approbation, there are some people out there who've never been on a plane in their lives, and never will be. Flying was a privilege, and one didn't take one's

79

privileges for granted.

But then two things happened, one quite slowly, the other far more quickly.

The first was that Burton Turnbo lived forty-seven years of comfortable middle class life. His belly had grown rounder, his myriad aches and pains complained around the clock, and his hairline was receding so fast it was on the cusp of breaking the sound barrier. The mid-life crisis he was certain he'd avoided snuck up behind him, cupped its clammy hands over his eyes and squawked 'guess who' in his ear.

If there was a silver lining to be found in this, it was that a mid-life crisis at forty-seven meant he could expect to live until nearly one hundred. Unfortunately, that silver lining had a great big cloud: economic stasis. Had he hit a ceiling? Was this all he could look forward to for another half a century? Was that something he even wanted?

And then the second thing happened: his wife, Thelma, got a promotion. Made partner at her law firm, in fact, which as far as Burton could tell meant she got her name on the front page of the firm's website instead of two or three clicks deep. And, of course, the promotion came with a fairly substantial bump in pay.

Burton had never expected to be the primary breadwinner the way his father and most of his male friends were. Yes, he was a well-liked, well-paid mathematics professor at a well-respected community college, but those 'well's were relative. Ultimately, he could cover about forty percent of their modest suburban expenses, while Thelma saw to the other sixty. Burton was used to being out-earned. Which was lucky, because not long after her promotion, Thelma started talking about finding a slightly nicer place to live.

Burton thought this was a swell idea, even if it would mean the percentage of the household that was 'his' would be shrinking. Being an enlightened, twenty-first century man, Burton was okay with this. He knew this to be true because he kept telling himself that it was.

I am okay with this, he would think when his wife went straight for the second-cheapest bottle of wine on the menu, instead of the cheapest.

I am okay with this, he reminded himself as his wife mentioned that she'd signed them up for the latest streaming service just to watch one dumb show.

I am okay with this, he determined through a smile as his wife handed him a hardcover copy of the book he'd expressed interest in after hearing it had just come out in paperback.

He *had* to be okay with it, because he knew Thelma had nothing but love in her heart. She wasn't lording the money over him, she wasn't trying to use it as a lever to shift the dynamics of their relationship, she wasn't acting any differently than she always had. Generosity and selflessness had always been her thing. It was just that now she had the means to match her ruthless decency.

When it came time to plan their summer vacation to Australia, the agreement was that Thelma would cover the expenses of the trip itself, and Burton would pick up the cost of travel. So he scrimped and saved (more a gesture than a necessity, as he and his wife pooled their finances) and surprised her by shelling out for first class tickets.

And the tickets *did* surprise her, quite pleasantly so.

Enjoying the illusion of having provided in a way he had not, Burton bundled away the not-so-secondary reason for getting the first class tickets; he'd have rather passed another 5mm kidney stone than spend fifteen hours entombed in a child's car seat.

Also, he wanted to do a nice thing for Thelma. But if having extra leg and shoulder room happened to be a tag-along benefit of that nice thing, well, so much the better.

And so, they'd settled into their spacious, cushy seats around 9PM, buckled up, lay back and relaxed. An older blonde flight attendant brought them each a glass of champagne, and Burton and Thelma toasted to their first ever first class flight.

"May it be the first of many," Thelma said as she took a sip of her bubbly.

"*Mhm*," Burton replied. The champagne giggled all the way down his throat, as though endlessly amused by the mantra he intoned even as he sat in the seat he himself had purchased: *I am okay with this.*

Before Burton went to sleep, he slipped off the loose-fitting New Balance sneakers he always wore to the airport. They weren't fancy, but they were comfy as all get out, and looked pretty damn slick to boot. Not that he was trying to impress anybody. The idea was to wear something loose and make getting through security as painless as possible. But it now occurred to him, with such generous legroom at his disposal, that he could slip them off for the flight and make fists with his toes, like in the movie.

So he did, and then slipped himself off into a pleasant dream in which he was a marquee hero, before the plane had even left the gate.

He awoke five hours later needing to pee, quite badly. Fortunately, the 'fasten seatbelts' sign was off. So he hoisted himself out of his aisle seat, pleased at not needing to disturb Thelma's awkward window-pillow slumber, and shuffled himself three rows forward. There beckoned the *exclusive* first class bathroom, unoccupied. Such a quick commute!

It was with a slight twinge of disappointment that he discovered the first class bathroom wasn't all he'd cracked it up to be.

He hoped the water on the floor had slopped off of somebody's hands, which he hoped were wet because they'd washed them. The alternative, which he was currently blasting into the bowl, might well compel him to File A Complaint, something he absolutely hated doing.

Because that would be, he thought with a smile and a flush, a very first class thing to do.

With a great sucking of the gut, he yanked the bifold door of the bathroom inwards and squeezed himself out. Alternating unwashed hands on other people's headrests, he plodded three rows back to his seat (bracing once for a rogue jolt of turbulence). He lowered himself into his seat and stretched, a big idiot grin plastered across his face. This was dangerous – he could see himself getting used to this kind of living. How had he ever managed to fly back in the trash compactor that was coach?

Not that the *people* in coach were the trash, obviously. He had been one of those people. He *was* one of those people. He just happened to be in first class now. This once. Whatever.

Leaning his head back into the pillowed headrest, which was downright sensual in its yield, he closed his eyes and drifted away.

He drifted right back and opened his eyes again, looking down at the well of his seat. He had all the room in the world in which to stretch out his feet. Nope, there was nothing in his way save his trendy-but-affordable satchel that he'd stuffed right under the ass of the traveler in front of him.

Nothing else.

Certainly not a pair of well-loved blue-and-gold New Balance sneakers.

Burton leaned forward, craning his neck to peer down under the seat in front of him. He pulled out the satchel. Nothing there.

Above him, the fasten seatbelt sign was still off. He reached down to unbuckle himself, pawing at his crotch for several seconds before remembered that he'd never rebuckled. Fortunately, his wife was still asleep, as were the three folks across the aisle to his right. There would be no witnesses to this pointless comedy.

Joints snapping and groaning, Burton dropped to his knees like a shipwrecked hull finally reaching the ocean floor. He fished his phone out of his pocket (quickly turning it onto airplane mode, which he'd forgotten to do prior to zonking out) and clicked on the flashlight. Unforgiving white light blasted the space under the seat in front of him, splitting the shadows in wide arcs, a watchtower in search of an escaped prisoner.

Calves now all the way out into the center of the aisle, left arm stabilizing himself on his own seat, he turned and shined his light into the storage space that lay directly under *his* ass, but belonged to the young child seated behind him (he'd always felt it odd that one's seat belonged to the person behind one, as much as it did to oneself).

There was a bag under there, a loud and colorful satchel that no doubt bore the visage of Thomas the Tank Engine, or Babar, or whatever kids were into nowadays. But no shoes.

"Excuse me," came a voice from over his shoulder. It was another flight attendant, not the one who had given him champagne but a much younger buck who was the kind of bald that happened by choice. He was pushing a drink cart, and seemed to be wondering if he could plow it right over Burton's obstructive calves and no-shoe, wet-socked feet.

"Oh, right," Burton mumbled as he heaved himself back to his feet. "Sorry."

"Is everything alright?" The man sounded genuine as

he asked this, but never took his eyes from the space Burton had only just ceased occupying.

I'm not a first class twit, Burton reminded himself. *I'm not about to File A Complaint. Besides, this is an airplane in mid-flight over the Pacific Ocean. It's not like the shoes could have gotten very far.*

Burton offered a half-cocked thumbs up as he plopped back down into his seat. "Yep, I'm good. Thought I lost something. Sorry about that."

The flight attendant smiled the smile of a sports mascot. "Not a problem, sir. Let me know if there's anything we can help you with. Would you like anything?"

"No," Burton replied with more frustration than he'd been aware of feeling. "I'm good."

"Ok." The attendant turned to the sleeping triumvirate on the other side of this aisle, and pushed the cart forward again.

With a convulsive jerk, Burton spun in his seat. "Oh wait, when you said 'anything' you meant 'a drink'."

The young man turned around slowly. Burton saw his customer service face being assembled piece by piece. "Yes, I meant a drink."

"Oh. Sorry. Um. Whiskey?"

"What kind?"

"Is there a price difference between them?"

The man betrayed the slightest hint of irritation, which Burton found admirable. Having never worked customer service in his life, he had never developed that talent for repression. *I must look like a stingy rich oaf to him,*

HAS ANYBODY SEEN BURTON'S SHOES?

Burton realized. Hadn't he often chuckled at the way rich folks could pinch pennies far more tightly than those for whom pennies actually mattered? How to let the flight attendant know that he wasn't that kind of guy?

"I'd like the most expensive whiskey you have," he announced, catching only too late how that might not be the quickest way to establish his common man bona fides.

"They're all the same price. Eight dollars."

"Oh. Well, give me whichever one *tastes* cheaper." And so the pendulum swung back the other way. Perhaps a more direct approach would do: "I'm not a wealthy man."

The flight attendant nodded agreeably, implying the placatory *of course you're not* one might expect to hear blasted through megaphones at small men on high ledges.

Burton finally decided to keep his mouth shut until he could fill it with bourbon. He wanted nothing more than to go back to sleep – the screen on the seatback in front of him told him he had about ten hours left on this trip.

But how could he be expected to sleep without knowing where his shoes were? It wasn't as though they would magically reappear beneath the seat in front of him if he went back to sleep. Would they? No, probably not. But they'd been there when he went to the bathroom – of this, he was almost positive.

So what had happened to his goddamned shoes?

He poured the proffered booze into the empty glass of ice he'd been given with it, and took a hearty pull. This time, there was no giggling on the way down his throat. It just burned.

Thelma first stirred when she heard the overhead luggage compartment slam shut. Even with the pillow as buffer, the heavy THWUNK travelled along the carriage of the plane and used her skull as grounding.

She second stirred when Burton placed a soft hand on her shoulder and gave it a few gentle wiggles.

"Thelma," he whispered at her.

Thelma offered her most articulate "Hrn?" as reply.

"Thelma, have you seen my shoes?"

"Hhm. M'dreaming."

"Thelma, honey."

"Mrm…hn…"

"*Thelma.*"

"Whar?" She peeled her head from the pillow and wiped a glaze of drool from her chin. "Have we landed?" She looked to the screen in the seatback in front of her. Ten hours remaining. Thelma turned to ask her husband a very reasonable question with her eyebrows.

"My shoes are gone."

Thelma rubbed her eyes and looked down at his feet, her bleariness (and so the likelihood of a speedy return to slumber) receding with every second. "How did that happen?"

"I took them off, then I got up to go to the bathroom, and when I got back, they were gone!"

"...why couldn't you take your shoes to the bathroom with you? On your feet," she clarified.

"I'd already taken them off. I didn't want to put them back on."

She shook her head. "You took your shoes off?"

"Yes."

"..."

"I thought it would be more comfortable."

"And they were there when you woke up?"

"Yeah. I'm almost positive. Now they're not. I've looked everywhere for them. Under the seats, in my bag, in the overhead luggage, everywhere. They're nowhere."

"Well, they have to be *somewhere*. It's not like somebody could run off with them. They're still on the plane."

"*I know*," Burton sulked. "Did you see anything?"

"I was asleep."

Half-turning, he gave her a skeptical side-eye. When this elicited no confessions, he leaned back and folded his arms. "I really need those shoes."

"Well, let's ask the flight attendants," Thelma suggested as she reached up and poked the little button above her seat. The reading light went on. "Whoops," she chuckled to herself as she found the button she was after all along. The airplane rewarded her perseverance by saying *bing!* and turning on a little blue light. "And, absolute worst case scenario, we can just get you another pair of sh-"

"*I know you can*," Burton snapped. At least he had the

decency to look almost as taken aback by the mild outburst as Thelma was. She opened her mouth to reply,
but before she could highlight the distinction of which
they were both well aware, the flight attendant who'd
brought them the champagne shuttled over, leaning on
the back of the seat in front them.

Just another example of the erosion of personal space, Burton
thought bitterly on behalf of the fast-asleep flyer in
front of him.

"How can I help you this evening?" the attendant
chirped.

"Somebody took my shoes," Burton replied. He'd
thus far resisted conjuring up a villain in the story of the
vanishing footwear, but it was hard to conceive a version of this tale that didn't involve a twirled mustache.

Instantly, the attendant's posture straightened. She
looked down at Burton's feet, and back into his eyes.
"How can you b-"

"They were here when I went to the bathroom. I
took them off," he interjected in the face of the attendant's confusion, "left them here, and went to the
bathroom. I took them off *earlier*, not to go to the bathroom. When I went to the bathroom, they were here. I
got back and they were not. I've looked everywhere for
them. *Everywhere*. They're not anywhere they could have
gotten without somebody putting them there."

She paused, and reflected. "What did they look like?"

"They *do* look like sneakers, New Balance sneakers.
Blue and gold. They're very cool," he added solemnly,
as though this would intensify the search.

The attendant turned to Thelma. "Did you see anything?"

"I was as-"

"She was asleep," Burton interrupted. "Did you see anything, by any chance?" He was clearly doing his best to keep calm.

Thelma knew perfectly well that was never a good sign, when Burton was *clearly* doing his best to keep calm.

"I'm sorry sir, but I didn't."

"Would you please ask your colleagues if they saw anything suspicious occurring at or around this seat?"

"I will, sir. I'll be right back. We'll do our very best to sort out this misunderstanding as soon as possible."

"Thank you," Burton growled as he took another nip of whiskey.

Off went the attendant. Burton swallowed, sighed, and turned to Thelma. "I'm sorry I'm being ornery. I'm just tired, and not really in the mood for this. It's just... *frustrating*. The shoes are *on* the plane. Somebody is just going to sit there, with *my* shoes, for ten hours."

"I know," she cooed, clumsily trying to snake her arm behind his head to run her fingers through his hair. That tended to sooth him. "It's alright. You're not being ornery. Everybody understands."

Burton smiled warmly at her, and hoped that this would all resolve itself smoothly.

That would be a short-lived hope.

"Sir?" Nancy the blonde flight attendant wilted slightly under Burton's glare. His was a look she had confronted countless times in first class; a pinchfaced grimace adopted by those whose privilege left them perpetually dissatisfied, but whose breeding prevented them from vocalizing that dissatisfaction. "I'm sorry, sir, but nobody on the cabin crew saw anything they would describe as suspicious."

"Oh? Are there cameras we can check, then?"

"Cameras inside the aircraft?"

The angry man's wife delicately placed her hand on his arm, which told Nancy that this was the kind of man who would happily have retorted *No, on the outside.*

Burton was glad Thelma had placed a hand on his arm, because he could feel the words *No, on the outside* scorching their way up his throat like whiskey that had gotten turned around.

He took a deep breath and plastered a boomerang smile on his face, knowing full well it would be returning to a frown before too long. "Oh, I suppose you don't have those. That's quite alright. I was just wondering. Is there any chance you could have the captain make an announcement? Perhaps whoever took the shoes could quietly bring them up to you, and you could return them to me, no questions asked. Er, they would give them to you no questions asked. There wouldn't be any questions about you returning them to me."

Nancy hesitated for a bit too long, blinked one too many times. "That's a wonderful idea, sir. As we get further into the flight, and more of the passengers have woken up, I'll get on th-"

"I don't want to wait that long. I won't be able to sleep without my shoes."

"I understand that, sir, but I can't wake up the entire plane to ask them if they've seen your shoes."

"Why not?"

"Because it wouldn't be fair to the rest of the passengers."

"Well it's not fair to me that my shoes have been stolen."

"I understand that, sir. But you're just one person."

Burton was gratified to see Nancy's face drop right after the word *just* – she knew that was the word she would most regret. He hoped to prove her right. "What's your name?"

"Nancy."

"What's your *last* name?"

"I'm not required to give you that, sir."

"Okay," was all he said, and turned away from her.

Nancy hovered for a moment. The angry man's wife favored her with that other look so common to first class, the spouse's wordless apology. Smiling her most magnanimous smile, Nancy turned and walked off to warn her fellow flight attendants about the man in seat 4B.

Thelma tried to stop Burton, but he just kept turning around and saying "they're on the *plane*, Thelma. My shoes are *on* the *plane*."

Burton swung out of his seat, and loomed over the poor sap in the seat in front of him. It was an older woman whose coke-bottle glasses were surely large enough to count as a carryon.

She didn't look like the sort of person who'd steal Burton's sneakers, but then again, that was sexist. It was the twenty-first century. *Anybody* could steal his sneakers.

He debated taking a head-on approach, hoping to startle the truth out of the old bag. *Where'd you put my sneakers!?* But that wouldn't do. After all, what if she *hadn't* been the one to take them? Burton didn't want to tip off the real culprit that he was onto him...

Or her...Could be anybody...

"Excuse me," Burton mewled. He didn't want to touch the woman; physical contact with strangers opened one up to all sorts of legal action, especially when the stranger looked like she was being held together by denture glue and prayers. "Excuse me, ma'am?"

The woman stirred, but didn't awaken.

He felt a hand on his shoulder, and immediately plotted the legal action he might take. He turned to see Thelma, looking concerned. "Please just sit down. *You* can buy another pair, we'll, I mean *you* can use the plane's Wi-Fi and buy them now, have them shipped right to the hotel."

"*I* bought these shoes. I've had them for years. They're my shoes. They're cool shoes and they're my shoes!" He turned back to the old woman. "HEY."

She awoke, just in time to see Burton's face melt

back into a gooey good-neighbor grin. "Oh, I'm sorry," she mumbled. "Was I snoring?"

"No-ho-ho," Burton stretched into a labored chuckle, "nothing of the sort. I was just wondering if you happened to have seen, or otherwise know the whereabouts of, a pair of New Balance sneakers. They belong to me."

The woman winced as she shifted in her seat, the better to face Burton. "I can't say I did. I'm sorry to say."

Burton pointed to the old man sitting next to her, displaying remarkable flexibility for his age in having fallen asleep with his head tucked practically between his legs. If the plane went down, he could just keep on snoozing; he was already in the crash position. "What about him?"

"That's my husband," the old woman smiled back at Burton. She was either oblivious to the slight tremor in the pointing finger, or was determined to conquer the fire behind it by keeping her cool. "He's still asleep."

Burton grimaced at them, until Nancy came clomping back down the aisle. "You need to leave your fellow travellers alone, Sir."

"Oh, it's alright," the old woman said to Nancy with maddening tranquility. Burton resented her for standing up for him, and couldn't begin to guess why. "He's just lost his footwear."

"That's *right*," Burton piled on, never one to shirk even the most unwelcome of allies.

"We are all well aware of the situation," Nancy

reminded him in her most peremptory tone, "but you must return to your seat."

"Why? The fasten seatbelt sign isn't on, is it? I'm free to get up and move about the cabin, aren't I?"

Nancy turned and gave a nearly imperceptible nod towards the front of the plane, and turned back to Burton. "Not if you're going to be disturbing people just trying to sleep through a flight."

Thelma weaved her way out into the aisle, taking Burton by the shoulders. "Come on."

Burton shook her off. "Like I've been disturbed? Someone on this flight has my shoes. They are *on* the *plane!*"

"Sir, do not raise your voice at me."

Thelma gripped him again, this time far tighter. "You're making a scene," she hissed in his ear. "Sit *down.*"

Bing! Bing! the plane concurred, as the fasten seatbelts signs lit up like a hundred bright ideas. There was a distinct lack of clicking and clacking, a pronounced absence of seatbelts being fastened. Nearly everyone on the plane remained fast asleep, buckled snugly.

Burton turned to Nancy in both awe and anger, as though she'd just made a beloved pet disappear, and then announced she wasn't sure how to bring it back. "You did that f-"

"There's going to be turbulence, Sir. Please sit down as fasten your seatbelt."

"How do I know *you* didn't take my shoes? You or one of the other *stewardesses?*" Burton uttered this last word as an epithet. Nancy was only too happy to accept it as one.

"Do you think a pair of sneakers is worth all the trouble you're causing? If one of us had taken them, we'd have given them back by now."

"Why? When you could just keep them? You're all above suspicion. The perfect crime!"

"Burton, that's *enough*." Thelma pulled him back towards his seat, not at all gently. "I'm so sorry," she added to Nancy.

"Not your fault," Nancy replied without taking her eyes from Burton.

He looked from his wife to the flight attendant to his wife to the flight attendant to his wife. "This is insane."

"Yes," Nancy agreed, "it is." She steeled herself for the greatest challenge a flight attendant faces: being demur in the face of a bully. "If you could just please resume your seat, I'll bring you a complimentary night-cap. When you and the rest of the passengers wake up, I'll make an announcement to the plane. As I said, we will do everything in our power to return your sneakers to you."

"They are *on* the *plane*," Burton whimpered.

"I know. I know."

Well-versed in knowing an opening when she saw one, Thelma negotiated Burton back into his seat, buckled his seatbelt, and ordered him another whiskey. By the time Nancy came back with it, Burton was sleeping.

When Burton woke up for the second time, the seatback before him boasted of only three hours left in the flight. Three hours in which the sneaker-swiping scoundrel need only hold her (or his) peace, in order to see her (or his) fiendish scheme through to completion.

Making a quick survey of the cabin, Burton saw a considerable majority of the passengers were awake. Nancy could defer the announcement no longer.

Burton shot his hand up and jammed the blue call button (*bing!*) hard enough to light up his own finger. He hardly felt the pain, though; he would have time to feel things when he had his sneakers back. Until then...

"Yes, Sir?" Nancy sounded exactly as exhausted as she was. Years of flight attending had taught her the art of the liminal doze, but on some shifts it came down to a choice between napping or caffeinating. She'd opted for the latter in this case, much to the detriment of her patience.

Burton, hale and hearty on a preposterous amount of rest, bored into her with his boring brown eyes. "You said you'd make an announcement when everybody was awake. Everybody's awake. Please make an announcement now."

Nancy sighed. "My pleasure."

As she shuttled out of Burton's sight, the man of the hour turned back to his wife, who was smiling as tolerantly as she could. "Is she going to make an annou-"

Bing! Bing! "Attention everyone." Nancy's voice sounded as though it was coming to them live from the cargo hold. How would anybody understand what she was saying? *"One of your fellow passengers has managed to misplace the shoes he wore onto the plane."* Burton did not care for that tone at *all*. *"They're blue and gold New Balance sneakers. If anybody sees them, or has any information as to their whereabouts, please notify one of the flight attendants immediately. You may provide the lead we need, to solve the crime of the century. Ugh,"* Nancy concluded as she re-racked the intercom. The huddles of laughter from throughout the plane were probably gratifying, but not enough to make up for the petty torture Burton hoped to inflict on her.

Thelma, perhaps smelling the blood in the water, shook her head on an ever-descending arc until she was looking at her lap.

"Did you hear that?!" Burton croaked beside her. "She mocked me! And then people *laughed!* Do they think this is funny? One of them took my shoes!" Eyes locked in her lap, head still shaking, Thelma placed a hand on her cheek as though she expected one or both to shatter at any second.

"They're not laughing at *you*, honey. They're laughing at the situation. Which is…unusual. You'd probably find it funny, if it were somebody else's sneakers that had gone missing."

"Been *stolen*. And no, I wouldn't."

"Burton. Please. Let's just let them go. You've got another pair in your bag, right? You can wear those, and this can be just a funny story to tell the clerk at the sneaker store or whatever." She finally lifted her head to look her defeat in the eyes. "Please."

"No," he replied reflexively. "You're not buying me

ano-"

"I don't want to buy you another pair! You can buy your own damn shoes!"

"With whose money, hm?"

Thelma felt as though she'd done more head shaking on this flight than in the rest of her life combined. "You assured me that you were perfectly comfortable with my earning more than you. If you aren't then we can discuss ways to assuage your disquiet."

Burton harrumphed and folded his arms. "Don't get lawyerly with me, Thelma. Not right now."

"Let's say you get your shoes back. Then what? When we get to the hotel, are you going to begrudge every purchase we make because it'll have been primarily my money covering the cost? Are you going to refuse to sleep in the bed, or breathe through the snorkel, or look at the koalas, just because I paid for the tour package?" She shifted in her seat. "What if I groused and grumbled the whole flight because you paid for this seat? And hell, how do we even adjudicate who paid for what? We have a joint account! It's all academic!" Settling down again, Thelma lowered her voice and placed a hand on Burton's shoulder, thrumming with tension as it was. "We love each other. We have a joint bank account *because* we love each other. That's all there is to it. This isn't a contest. It's not *my* money that would be buying the shoes, or *your* money. It's *our* money."

Burton considered this for a moment. "But they're *my* shoes."

HAS ANYBODY SEEN BURTON'S SHOES?

"No," she replied despite her better judgment, "now they're somebody else's."

Burton looked at, into and through her. Once upon a time, when they were both young and struggling, Burton had been the most generous man Thelma had ever met. Few and far between were the nights when she got to treat him – either he would snatch the check before she could even glimpse the total, or else he would insist on going dutch. Thelma had always considered this a mark of his innate kindness, but in hindsight she couldn't help but wonder if she should have seen it for the bright, flashing warning sign that it ended up being. There were generous men in the world, and then there were men who went through the motions of kindness, because that was one of the last socially acceptable outlets for their condescending brand of chivalry. Was there a way to tell one from the other? And were they mutually exclusive?

Thelma loved her husband. About this, she had no doubt. But he could also be a real dickhead, no doubt about that either.

Three hours later, a loud *clunk* announced their arrival. The lights came on, and everyone shot to their feet. Or, more to the point, to their shoes.

Burton remained seated, by force of habit. He was used to being farther back in the cabin, waiting several minutes for the people in front of him to debark. When he recalled the final privilege of this ill-advised act of class infiltration, he still remained seated.

Next to him, Thelma stood up, saw her husband lost in distant meditations, and sat back down. There the Turnbos remained, until the entire plane had debarked.

"Very sorry, Sir, but it's time to get off the plane." That was Nancy, half-crouched with her hands clamped onto her knees, like someone telling a child an unconvincing lie.

"We never found my shoes," he sulked. "They were *on* the *plane*."

"Very sorry, Sir. Better luck next time."

Burton scowled up at her, but said nothing. The fight was out of him. It was over. The shoes were gone.

Some people at baggage claim turned at snickered at Burton. *Yes*, he thought, *laugh it up*. He had no doubt that one of those fat faces with their feminine laughs and low-class cargo shorts was amused less by a general sense of shadenfreude, and more by the blue-and-gold, size ten and a half secret bundled away in their dumbass little rolly-bag...

"None of you happen to have my shoes, do you?" he asked in a hang-dog voice he hadn't heard coming from his mouth since one of his students corrected him in the middle of a lecture three years ago.

A few more scattered chuckles, now embellishments in a still-life of pity. Derision would have been preferable to pity. Good grief.

The baggage carousel gave a honking laugh of its own and spun to life. As they waited for their bags to tumble onto the belt, Burton mumbled an apology to his wife. She smiled and threw an arm around his shoulder. "It's alright. Next time just talk to me if you're uncomfortable with something, you know?"

"Mhm." He retrieved his own arm from his side and threw it over top Thelma's shoulder, squeezing tight. "But really, I'm not uncomfortable with anything. I'm comfortable with everything."

Thelma sighed, but kept her arm around her husband, thinking about warning signs she'd missed in the past, and moments she might be coming back to ten years from now in a similar mindset.

For the record: the old man whose wife was awoken by Burton in the early moments of the search? He took the sneakers. He saw them poking out from beneath his wife's legs, and liked the look of them. After a lifetime of loafers he had sworn off uncomfortable footwear for good. The sneaks looked snug, so he snagged 'em. And why not? He had paid for his first class ticket with funds embezzled from a mid-tier property insurance company, so filching a pair of sneakers was *nothing* to him.

As luck would have it, they were too small. So he threw them out and forgot about them.

Eleven months later, Burton and Thelma Turnbo got a divorce. Thelma represented herself. She offered to help Burton find a good lawyer at another firm. He declined with colorful language and elected to represent himself as well.

IDENTICAL PIGS

With the money she won, Thelma took another vacation. She flew coach.

what happens after james t. kirk eats too much taco bell

captain's clog

what do you call a dog in an underwater vessel

a subwoofer

what do you call a rabbi's angry outburst

a temple tantrum

FOR PLAYERS 2-4

"It's actually really fun," Marty reassured them as he heaved the box off the top shelf. The weight of it sent him staggering backwards a step, but he recovered quickly.

Beth frowned at this, as she had frowned at so much of the evening. At some point last week, her fiancé Isaac had reconnected with an old high school buddy. That would be Marty. It had been a chance meeting, the kind where one person spots the other in a grocery store and calls their name in the keening register of a fighter jet going supersonic and feeling a bit embarrassed about it. The spotter – in this case Marty – then sidesteps their way up to the spottee, echoing their initial call until they receive a response. According to Isaac, his response was "Hey!...?", and then a generous silence inviting Marty to identify himself.

When reenacting this story for Beth, Isaac had portrayed Marty as a half-man-half-pigeon. "Marty!? It's me, Marty!" he had squawked through bared teeth. Beth had laughed at that. Isaac told her a few stories about Marty, some dweeb from his Conshahawken days that he had completely forgotten existed. Vice-President of the A/V club, star mathlete, runner-up in the spelling bee, stuff like that. A run of the mill loser too unambitious to qualify as 'eccentric', Marty didn't even stand out enough to get bullied. A born seat-filler, that was the Marty of Isaac's description.

So Beth's gob was well and truly smacked to discover, just a few days after that whole derisive low-down, that her presence was expected for a double-date board game night. At Marty's house. On a *Friday*.

"You told me he's boring," Beth protested. "You literally didn't say a single nice thing about him."

Isaac shrugged. "I said *he* was nice, didn't I?"

"Nice is what you say about people when you can't think of anything nice to say about them."

Another shrug, because that was true.

A man of many shrugs, that was Isaac. This was the core of both Beth's love of, and frustration, with her man. He rarely-to-never lost his temper nowadays, opting instead for white-knuckle equanimity. It looked effortless from the outside, but Isaac had confided to Beth just how great a challenge it was for him to keep the lid on. Young Isaac had been a furious boy, and it took some perspective-shifting incidents in college to make clear how little patience the world had for a furious man. So he went to therapy, took up meditation, and broke off a toxic, long-term relationship. By the time Beth met him in grad school, Isaac had found inner peace, and tackled it to the ground.

Of course, sometimes that hard-won agreeability made for a passive partner. Which meant Beth getting conscripted into loathsome social engagements that *neither* wanted to attend, but that Isaac hadn't the gall to turn down.

Like game night with some little dweeb from Isaac's gradeschool days.

On the one hand, a single night sacrificed to mandatory fun wouldn't be the end of the world. On the other hand (clad in a powerful, filigreed gauntlet), this wasn't a single night. This was one night of many similar impositions, and Beth had just about had enough. "I really got the impression you didn't like him," she pressed.

"Why?"

"The voice you did. '*Hi, I'm Marty!*'"

Isaac laughed.

"See?!"

"He was a nice kid."

Beth sighed.

And now here they were, at Marty's. And there he was, heaving a game off the shelf. Sorry, not a game – a *chore*. It was one of those ruthlessly complicated parodies of fun, the kind with hardcover instructions and fifteen dice.

"Ooh," Beth tried, pointing to the shelf, "is that Balderdash I see?"

Lea, Marty's 'girlfriend' (who seemed about as comfortable as somebody on a blind date, still waiting to meet the mystery man), bobbed her head up and down. "Yeah! We've got all the best games. We love board games, but it's so hard to play the best board games with only two people."

She looked to Marty for reassurance, but his concentration was fully engaged with the ferrying of the monstrous box over to the table.

"Yeah," Isaac agreed. "Most games say you can play with just two players, but, like, there aren't really any that work with just two. Actually."

Beth was trying very hard not to frown. This was just Isaac being agreeable again, saying things that he knew would be well-received whether or not he agreed with them. She could think, off the top of her head, of four games they had in their apartment that the two of them had had a grand old time with. And that wasn't even counting a deck of cards.

"Jenga," she offered, just to stir the pot.

"Yeah!" Isaac agreed.

Beth opened her mouth to say something, but then Marty dropped the box on the table. It landed with a teeth-rattling *THUMP*. Everyone, even Marty, flinched.

"It's actually really fun," he repeated to Beth's evident incredulity. That's how you know a game is fun, when the pitch features the word *actually*.

The box was big enough to fit a picnic, without squishing the full loaf of bread even a little bit. Marty placed the pads of his fingers on either side and lifted. The lid only reluctantly left the box, parting with a depressurized sucking sound. Inside the box were all of Pandora's old friends, save the last.

Beth looked to the lid, which Marty placed at the edge of the table. No way it was staying there, with how much shit was in the box. Maybe that was the object of the game? See how much shit you could stack on the table?

That wouldn't explain the name, though.

"Chicken Fingers, Chicken Thumbs," she read off the lid.

"It's really fun," Lea echoed.

Isaac's elbow poked Beth in the side. She looked to him and got the classic *please be nice* face, intimately familiar to both of them. So she gave him the *you wouldn't have to be giving me that face if you didn't keep dragging me to stupid things with people you don't even like* face. To that, he replied with the *you know I fully subscribe to the 'selective friendship' philosophy, but it's harder for me to cut people off than it is for you* face. So Beth gave him the *be that as it may, here is where your reluctance to curate your social circle has gotten us: playing a game called Chicken Fingers, Chicken Thumbs with a kid you never even spoke to in school* face, which was a new face, but nonetheless perfectly comprehensible.

Oblivious to the facial exchange, Marty plowed ahead: "The object of the game is, well, I guess it's to *win…*" he left room for laughter, which Lea and Isaac gamely filled, "…ha, yeah, but the way you win is you have to hitchhike your chicken off of the farm and into the city." He lifted a board from the box, folded to a fourth its size, and handed it to Lea. She wrestled with it as he continued: "see, you have to use your chicken *thumbs*, to hitchhike, or you become chicken *fingers*." He pulled out a little rectangular box, perfectly sized for a pair of reading glasses, and handed that, too, to Lea. She opened it, poured out what appeared to be a small K'Nex set, and started assembling something.

Assembling. Beth just shook her head.

"So yeah," Marty said as he pulled yet another board from the box, this one a trifold which expanded into a pop-up pyramid, "basically, it's pretty simple once you get the rules down. There are three boards, and you first have to draw a card from the 'draw' pile," a pile he brandished from inside the box and placed inside the pyramid, "and that's from the coop." He tapped the triangle. It collapsed. He set to rebuilding it. "So you draw from the coop, just be careful because you can see it's a bit fragile, but you draw from it carefully and that tells you how many times to roll the dice. You can see it's *really* fragile." He tried to rebuild the coop again.

Isaac pointed to the contraption Lea was snapping into shape. It looked like a very small gallows. "What's that?"

"That, um, well, I'll get to that. That's where it gets complicated."

Beth once again looked over to the shelf of games, replete with accessible, enjoyable alternatives. "I don't know," she ventured as diplomatically as she could, "is anybody else in the mood for something a bit more, um, less? I see Scrabble over there." She favored Marty with a plaintive look. "Isaac tells me you did real well in a spelling bee!"

Marty paused for a moment, looking from Beth to

Isaac. "I can't believe you remember that!"

Isaac smiled and, of course, shrugged.

Marty returned to setting up the poultry-themed timesink.

Lea continued to be engrossed by the contraption she was still building.

Nobody made any acknowledgement of the Scrabble suggestion.

Beth closed her eyes and tried to find, if not her own happy place, then Isaac's. It was Friday night, an evening draped in gorgeous autumn violet. And here she was. Chicken Fingers, Chicken Thumbs.

The things she did for love.

"Buck buck B-KAWWWWK!" Marty flapped a few more times, then sat back down and moved his Chicken Fingurine forward two spaces.

In Chicken Fingers, Chicken Thumbs, clucking like a chicken was part of the game. What was truly despicable about this was that it served absolutely no function; it was a simple humiliation encoded into the instructions, intended to celebrate a particular sort of die-roll/card-draw combo.

Marty and Lea were *sticklers* for the rules.

They had been playing for two hours. Well, they had been *playing* for fifteen minutes. The remainder of that time had been dedicated to pouring over the instructions, attempting to start a game only to halt it, refer back to the directions, and restart, but this time for *real*. All the while, Marty assured them that it was fun.

Actually.

Beth had largely fallen silent by this point. She had a million other things she could be doing on a Friday night. She and Isaac could have gone dancing, or she could be at home with a good book. Even a bad book. Even a *cook*book.

Frustrated by her own surliness, Beth made yet another conversational overture, knowing full well it would be dashed upon the barren crags of Marty's anti-personality as all the others had been. Isaac, too, had been making similar efforts and met with similar disaster. Lea wasn't even trying. They were just sitting around, silently shuffling oversized action figures across a board and sometimes making chicken noises.

"So…" Beth scanned the room for common interests, finding nothing of use beyond an open box from 1-800-CONTACTS sitting on the table. "Which of you wears contacts?"

"Neither," Marty replied, pushing his glasses up his nose. "Lea's mom just shipped us some salt and pepper shakers, and she used that box to send them."

"BAWK BAWK BAWK," said Lea. She moved her Fingurine one space. Hardly worth clucking about, as far as Beth was concerned.

Silence once again reigned, as Isaac struggled to recall the proper order of his turn. He drew a card from the coop's draw pile, stuck it under the "Egg" pile, lifted the barnyard door, drew a card from the "Hatch" pi-

"You gotta roll the first die before you draw from

the Hatch pile," Marty reminded him.

"Oh, right." Isaac rolled the first die, which came up 'two'. So he drew two cards from the "Hatch" pile.

Marty watched Isaac's hands attentively, as though trying to figure out how a sleight of hand trick was done.

Isaac's turn went poorly, and thus, he did not cluck.

"You know," Marty mooned to Isaac as Beth took up the die, "I still can't believe you remembered I was in the spelling bee."

"'Course I do," Isaac replied.

Marty nodded gratefully. Beth drew from the coop's draw pile and said, "He also told me y-"

"It's best if you pay attention to your turn," Lea suggested.

Sensing a portentous trembling in the camel's back, Beth put her card down on the table. "Well then I'll just put the turn on hold, say what I was going to say and then resume. Is that alright?"

"It's irregular."

"Ok. What I was *saying*," she relayed to Marty, "was that Isaac also told me you were a star mathlete."

Marty blushed a bit. "Gosh, I don't know if I would say *star…*"

"Of course you were!" Isaac boomed. He seemed just as eager to have an actual conversation as Beth was.

"Well, alright. I was pretty good, anyway."

"Good at math *and* spelling," Beth marveled a bit more condescendingly than she meant to, "a double threat! I could barely find my way around either."

Marty's flush deepened, to a degree that might have alarmed a medical professional. "It's just that I worked hard on them, is all. I'm not special or anything!"

"And you were Vice-President of the A/V club?"

At this, Marty's hue darkened, his smile flatlining.

Isaac, uncharacteristically flustered, rose from his seat slightly. "*And* a regional champion at…that computer game, what was that computer game?"

"*Starcraft*," Marty mumbled.

Lea leaned forward and tapped Beth on the hand. "It's still your turn," she reminded her.

"Um…right." Watching Marty and Isaac from the corner of her eye, Beth finished out her turn. She moved her Fingurine forward three spaces and pushed the first board gently towards Marty.

He just stared at it.

And then, he kept staring.

"You have to cluck," he finally said, eyes still locked on the board.

Beth looked to Isaac. He seemed…well, it was hard to say what he seemed, but what he *didn't* seem was like the Isaac who'd gotten down on one knee and looked up with stars in his eyes. This Isaac looked…

Younger.

"You know," Lea prompted Beth. "BAWK BAWK BAWK?"

"Cluck cluck," Beth offered.

"You have to *mean* it," Marty groused. Where had all that good humor of his gone?

Beth sighed. "CLUCK CLUCK."

Marty grudgingly accepted this and began his turn.

Beth shot a *what the hell is so upsetting about A/V club?* face to Isaac, but he wasn't looking. His face was unfamiliar, unreadable.

Marty moved his piece forward one square. He did not cluck.

"Marty," Isaac said.

Marty looked up.

"You need to fucking get over it."

Beth and Marty both boggled at Isaac. Lea paid as much attention as she could to her turn.

"It was three months off. Literally three months."

"I would have been president senior year," Marty fumed. "Instead I got stuck being VP again. As a *senior.*"

"BAWK BAWK BAWK," Lea crowed.

Isaac glared at Marty even as he pulled the first board towards him and reached towards the coop, which collapsed. As he struggled to rebuild it, he shook his head, which probably made the rebuilding harder. "And so what? What, did that follow you to college? It's haunted you and fucked up your life? What?"

"Noooo," Marty allowed, "but I was still pretty bummed about it!"

Seeing as they had been effectively put on mute, Beth felt safe directing a question to Lea: "do you know what they're talking about?"

"He's still very upset about it," Lea replied knowingly.

"About what?"

Lea pointed to the third board in the center of the table. "You have to draw a Cross The Road card," she told Isaac.

Isaac did as told, not taking his eyes off of Marty.

Beth didn't like what she saw in those eyes. Not stars. Black holes. She put a restraining hand on his arm, something she'd never had to do before. More often, the roles were reversed.

She had no idea what she was supposed to do.

The board went to Beth. She took her turn as quickly as possible.

"B-B-B-B-BAAAAAAAWK!" she screamed, hoping the absurdity of grumpy little Beth making such a racket might defuse some of the tensions.

It didn't work. All she'd managed to do was make herself look stupid.

"Isaac," she said. He finally broke away from Marty and turned towards her. "What's up?"

Marty ducked his head down and took his turn.

"What's *up*," Isaac said just above an indoor voice, "is that one time Marty made a video about everybody's favorite Halloween treats at school. I said 'blumpkin', he aired it, and got in trouble. But like barely. And," he added, directing this towards Marty, "it's not like I figured he'd actually *use* it. That's not *my* fault. It wasn't *live*."

"I didn't know what a blumpkin was," Marty snapped. "You should have told me."

"I didn't know you were editing it! I didn't know who was in the damn A/V club if they weren't in front of the camera!'"

"Buck buck B'KAAAAWK!" Marty slammed his Fingurine forward two spaces.

Beth watched, fascinated, as Lea snatched the board over to her and took her sweet time drawing a card from the coop. "What *is* a blumpkin?" she finally asked Isaac.

It was Marty who answered: "It's when a lady gives a man a…a…she gives him oral sex, while he's on the toilet. Defecating."

"A girl gives a guy a blowjob while he's taking a shit," Isaac clarified, "and he cums right at the same time he shits."

"…" Beth said. Then she laughed.

Isaac, the one she knew and loved, resurfaced for a moment. "It's funny, see?"

"That's so gross!"

"That's why I thought it was so funny! And it sounds like pumpkin!"

"Did you come up with that?"

"BAWK BAWK BAWK!" Lea pushed the board towards Isaac.

"No way. I just heard it and thought it was funny, because it was so gross."

Marty folded his arms. "Yeah, well, what a laugh, I put that video on the morning announcements, and I got kicked off the A/V club for the rest of the year. Then when I came back next year, freaking Willie Hill was president. A *junior*. And I got held back as Vice President. As a *senior*. *Willie Hill!*"

"UGH." Isaac rolled his eyes. "Who fucking cares, Marty?! That was like fifteen years ago! You're doing fine!"

"Yeah, well, I still think about it!"

"You're the only fucking one!!!"

Beth gave Isaac's arm a little squeeze. She had heard him talk about his old temper, but hadn't seen it in action before. Even still, she thought she recognized it in profile.

Marty, of course, would have caught him at just the right age to know the old Isaac. Maybe that's why he was shrinking backwards a bit now.

Sensing the shift, Isaac leaned a bit further forward. "I mean, Jesus dude, you don't even come to the reunions! You know how many people there talk about how you were Vice President of the A/V club as a *senior*, how embarrassing that was? NOBODY! Nobody talks about it because nobody talks about *you*, good or bad."

Beth squeezed his arm tighter. "You should really always pay attention to your turn," she advised him. She looked to Lea for moral support, but she was busy investigating her lap.

Isaac shook her hand off like it was a horsefly. He'd never done *anything* like that before. "*Hey,*" she rumbled

He tossed a "sorry" out of the corner of his mouth, eyes still fixed on Marty.

They both looked like they had lots more to say. Recriminations, unflattering reminiscences, culminating in a present-tense dick measuring contest. Who was making more money, who had more friends, who was happier in more measurable ways. Who had won the race to adulthood.

Beth couldn't help recalling that on the Chicken Fingers, Chicken Thumbs box, next to the FOR PLAYERS 2-4 tag, there was one that declared it a perfect game FOR AGES 6-13.

"Why would I want to come to one of those stupid reunions," Marty shot back, "partying and drinking and small-talking, when I could be, you know, doing *work*?"

"Doing work why, so you can buy more action figures? Beth, tell him how much we've traveled since I got my last raise."

"Cluck cluck," Beth replied. She stood up, marched into the kitchen, and helped herself to a short tumbler of wine. Shortly thereafter, Lea joined her and showed her where she kept the tall glasses.

They sipped in relative silence.

"So how did you and Marty meet?" Beth finally asked over the bickering coming from the living room.

Lea chuckled. "We met at a varsity volleyball game. He was filming. I guess he hoped they would use it, even though he was suspended from the club then. I mean, I hope that's why he was filming women's volleyball." That had the sound of a fossilized joke.

Beth took a thoughtful sip. "So it was sort of a good thing he kicked out of that club, right?"

"*I* thought so." A few more sips were sipped before the inevitable: "How about you and Isaac?"

"Grad school. *Well...*Tinder. Our mutual interest

was, ha, pilates. He seemed pretty chill."

Lea chuckled again, a bit deeper this time. "Pilates is like ab stuff, right?"

"Core, yeah."

"You keep up with it?"

Beth smiled and slapped her belly. "Nice of you to ask. No, I sort of fell off when we moved."

"How come?"

"There are so many fucking gyms in this city, I just can't be bothered to figure out which are good. Which is definitely funny, I get that."

"My gym is pretty good! They do pilates classes too, I think."

"Really? Is it expensive?"

"The membership's pretty usual for the area, I guess. I think the classes come with it, but I've never taken any. The gym's pretty good though!" She sipped. "I'm pretty sure I can get you into a class if I sign you in on a guest pass. If you want to check one out."

"No shit?"

"I think. If you wanted."

"That'd be awesome, yeah, I'd love that! Thank you!" Beth tried for another sip and found her glass empty. She presented her discovery to Lea, who just a few seconds later made a similar discovery regarding her own drinking situation.

So as the living room grew deafening with arguments about an outsize past, Beth and Lea took the wine, decamped to a bedroom and talked about small futures.

why did santa stop visiting the family that put a
christmas tree in their chimney

they were just a pine in the ass

what do you call a person who is crazy in their free time

a wackhobby

which prehistoric monument will soothe your sore
throat

lozhenge

BRAND MANAGEMENT

BRAND MANAGEMENT

It had been a pretty dope year, on account of all the dope shit that had occurred therein.

C-C-Craig's Way hit the airwaves at 6 P.M. on a Tuesday, and by Wednesday morning it was all anybody could talk about. Brydon Plyst – twice written off for his youth and his mid-tier YouTube reaction video channel – elicited some histrionic reactions of his own as the eponymous Craig Angel, a preternaturally talented genius-level speech pathologist who solves crimes using language and also is relatable and flawed because he stutters sometimes. The network, previously uneasy about wading into the increasingly crowded Original Content marketplace, was almost as elated by the reaction to *C-C-Craig's Way* as they were unprepared for it. And so they panicked, filling Brydon's schedule with three or four TV appearances per day for three straight weeks. It was a grueling blitz that would have snuffed out a lesser light, but Brydon burned bright. He worked the circuit like he was campaigning for president, flashing teeth (quickly endorsed by Colgate) and flipping hair (snapped up by Axe) at anything that even *looked* like a camera lens. By the time the fourth episode of *C-C-Craig's Way* aired, Brydon was a bona fide phenomenon, and a no-shit millionaire to boot.

And then, that December, he turned nineteen.

Pretty dope.

But in all that excitement, all of the appearances on *The Tonight Show* playing extremely hilarious games with Jimmy Fallon like "How Many Marbles" and "Now There Is A Band-Aid In Your Hair", all of the negotiations about the already-locked renewal of *C-C-Craig's Way*'s second season and how Brydon's paychecks would have to have a whole lot more zeroes on the end, all of the hot chicks who were falling all over themselves to play Twister with the Plyster…in the midst of the dope shit, Brydon had lost sight of what truly mattered.

Defining his brand.

C-C-Craig's Way's season finale was about to air, and it would be a few weeks yet before cameras rolled on season two. Brydon's agent had counseled him that actually eight commercials for six different products was probably enough for this month, but what did he know? Not as much as Brydon, who had already recorded reaction videos for every episode of *C-C-Craig's Way*, and uploaded them all in one go. Which the head of the Mrs. Fields Channel said was technically "leaking the season finale", but like, what was she so mad about, didn't she know how it ended?

And so he found himself in a lens-less purgatory. It

sucked. He was stuck at his parents' stupid brownstone in Boston, because the paperwork on his sick new Cali crib hadn't gone through yet or whatever. Even worse, he couldn't think of how else to keep his face in front of the world. He tried calling all of his new friends, like James Corden and Seth Meyers, but nobody was picking up. Stumped, Brydon caved and texted his plain old nobody-buddies from school to see what was good in the hood. He supposed that, in a pretty small way, they qualified as a part of the world.

His old buddies expressed disbelief that Brydon had emerged from his own asshole. While he did not appreciate the comment, Brydon tolerated it because that was what you did when you were still super down to earth. After the ribbing subsided and the reconnection began, it emerged that what was good in the hood was, as it had always been, Giustina Pizzeria.

An old-school hole in the wall with a charismatically churlish staff and a floor plan that had apparently been crumpled up into a little ball before construction began, Giustina Pizzeria had been home to many a fond memory for Brydon and his crew. It was a one-of-a-kind neighborhood institution (as long as you visited the original location), and on top of all that they slung a dope 'za.

So it was at Giustina Pizzeria that Brydon met his old buddies. Some of them, anyway.

"Where is everybody?" he asked the two friends who had shown.

Mike and TJ looked to each other, looked to the

space not being taken up by the three no-shows, and looked back to Brydon.

"*We're* right here," TJ grumbled.

Brydon considered the optics of this. Eating out at a restaurant with only two buddies, when five had been invited? Sure, there was no way for TMZ to find out that he'd been thrice jilted this eve…was there? They were really good at finding stuff like that…

Oh god, what if one of his so-called buddies sold Brydon's texts to the paparazzi? What would the headlines be? Look at Brydon "Two Friends" Plyst? Or, um…they'd probably do something super lame with C-C-Craig's Way, like they'd just totally roast him with a funny pun or something.

Brydon couldn't think of any. He really wanted to. So he just kept staring into space.

"HEY!" called a familiar sandblaster sing-song from the kitchen, "YOU COMIN' OR GOIN'?"

Mike and TJ's faces lit up.

"She's still here," Mike giggled.

That brought Brydon back. A literally million-dollar grin split his face. "Ooh, baby!" The love of his life! Giustina!

This was, of course, a joke that was funny because this woman was a.) not named Giustina, b.) old and c.) fat. Even *before* he was Brydon Plyst, Brydon would absolutely never have stooped so low. This is why the joke was very funny.

It was *extra* funny now because he was rich and famous, so there was absolutely definitely no way in hell. He continued to pretend there was, for the sake of the very funny joke, because he was down-to-Earth.

"We're coming!" Brydon announced with a lewd waggle of his focus-tested eyebrows. Mike and TJ were properly amused.

The three pushed their way into the pizzeria and huddled into a booth. TJ sat on one side, Brydon on the other. Then Mike tried to slip in next to Brydon. So like, and what, it was just supposed to look like Brydon and Mike came to this North End dive to ask TJ if he knew a guy who knew a guy? Like it was *The Goodfella?* Not a chance. Not a *chance*.

"Dude," Brydon huffed at the table.

Mike paused, halfway to a seated position. "What?"

"Uh, gay much?"

From across the table, TJ sighed. "He wants you to sit over here," he translated.

Mike cocked his head towards TJ. "Really?" He swung back to Brydon. "Why?"

"He's big-timing us."

"No I'm not!" Brydon hissed, ever-vigilant for phone cameras peeking out of purses. "I've gotta think about fucking appearances now, guys. I'm sorry. I'm sorry I asked if you were gay much," he mumbled to Mike.

Mike shrugged. "It's all good, dude." He sat down next to Brydon again.

"Fuckingsitoverth-"

Mike shot up and shimmied in to TJ's side of the booth.

TJ folded his arms. "How's it look for you? Good fucking appearances?"

"Sure," Brydon mumbled. He'd gotten distracted by what truly mattered, what he'd lost sight of in all that excitement.

How many times had he and his *five* buddies staggered into Giustina Pizzeria and marveled at all the celebrity pictures on the walls, only sometimes ironically? You had your signed headshots, no big deal, but the bulk of the interior decoration was that pizza shop staple: low-quality snaps of celebrities standing next to the manager or whoever got to wear that big cauliflower hat. Each picture had its own ill-fitting emerald green frame, tessellating all over the walls like an invasive species. Brydon had always wondered how these come about. Do the celebrities approach the management and alert them to the opportunity? Do they take the picture in exchange for a free pie? Or do they wait for management to spot *them*? The big guns, your Leonardo DiCaprios or Scarlett Johanssons, the just-wait method was plausible. It'd be pretty damn hard to not realize you had a star crammed into your booth. But some of these faces, Brydon hadn't the slightest clue. What were the chances...whoever that was, "Rob Lowe", what were the chances that guy just popped in and got spotted? No way he didn't tip somebody off. *Hey, I'm famous, I'm...Rob Lowe, you want my picture?*

Pathetic. That wasn't how it was gonna go with Brydon. He was a DiCaprio, no doubt. A Johansson.

"This is gonna be really embarrassing," Brydon

blushed.

"What is?" TJ asked.

Brydon pointed to the pictures on the walls. "They're gonna come over and ask for my picture, say *oh my god, I saw y-*"

"Whaddyawant?" asked not-Giustina, who had just come whirling in from a Dick Tracy lineup. She was just as Brydon remembered her: Mount Rushmore's Roosevelt with makeup applied via tactical air strike.

"Hmmm…." Brydon deliberated. He had expected her to initiate The Spotting, to do a double-take and exclaim 'my goodness, you're Brydon Plyst!'

Come to think of it, he was quite surprised that nobody else in the establishment had shouted that sort of thing yet.

As he was considering if perhaps he ought to have shaved more carefully this morning, TJ brusquely put in their usual order: "two cheese pies, please."

"Sure," not-Giustina replied, as though TJ had just told her he was Sinatra reincarnated. And then she was gone.

Brydon reeled in her absence. He wasn't really expecting her to *fawn*, just…okay, maybe get a bit weak in the knees. Acknowledge him at the very *very* least! He was a bona fide phenomenon, for heaven's sake!

"Do you think she didn't recognize me?" Brydon fished. He noted only after he'd finished asking the question that he had interrupted a conversation between Mike and TJ. "What were you guys just talking about?"

As they had so many times, Mike and TJ looked knowingly at each other. Back at Brydon. "Are you on drugs?" TJ inquired.

"The fuck kind of a question is that?"

Mike hugged his elbows. "You've been acting weird. People on TV do drugs. Sometimes."

"Not me," Brydon declared. "I don't do drugs."

"Alcohol is a drug," TJ smirked.

"No it's not."

"Yes it is."

Mike furrowed his brow. "It's illegal?"

TJ raised a professorial finger. "Not all drugs are illegal."

Brydon, no longer certain what point he was making, sniped "well alcohol *is* illegal for us until we're twenty-one."

"Why? What did we do?" Mike moaned.

Not-Giustina swung in with a pitcher of water. She shoved it in Brydon's face. "Here," she commanded, "hold this." And then she was gone.

Brydon held the pitcher in front of his scowl for several seconds. This was stupid. Why weren't they recognizing him? Why was he, television icon, teenage heartthrob, stuck here bickering with these hangers-on in a pizzeria where nobody recognized him?

Why wasn't he on the wall yet? How did…"Rob Lowe" make the cut and *Brydon Plyst* didn't?

He gently laid the pitcher down on the table. Mike and TJ were off talking about something that nobody cared about, a girl that one of them was trying to ask out or something. Whatever. Either they would break up, or one or the other would die. It wouldn't last.

But a picture in a frame? That was the kind of thing heroes in apocalypse movies find in their childhood homes. The windows are blown out and there are vines everywhere and all of the furniture is upside down, but no matter how dramatic the cataclysm, there always remains a picture in a cracked frame to be wistfully examined.

Why not his?

The pizzas came and they ate. Brydon shoveled the slices in silence.

Maybe they just weren't expecting someone of his stature to be slumming it in a neighborhood pizza dive? The sheer cognitive dissonance of his being here was rendering him invisible.

All they needed, in that case, would be a little nudge.

A different woman, younger and even more plump than not-Giustina, brought the check.

Brydon slammed his hand down on the bill. "I got this," he announced.

Mike seemed happy about that, but TJ just rolled his eyes. "We can split it like we always do," he averred. "It's really not that much."

"No, no, I got it." Brydon pulled out his wallet, slipped out a card and laid it on the edge of the table with the check. "I wanna get it. 'Cuz I had such a fun-ass time tonight."

"You didn't even say anything."

"…yeah I did."

"Barely."

"You were mostly eating your 'za," Mike piled on.

Brydon felt his shoulders ticking up towards his ears. "Yeah, we were all just eating our 'zas! They're fucking good-ass pies!"

TJ waved his thumb between himself and Mike. "*We* had a whole conversation."

"Oh, yeah? About *what*?"

"You weren't even *listening*!"

"I was…" Brydon looked down and saw that the check, and his card, had vanished. "Wait, did you guys see who picked that up?"

"A lady. I think she worked here?" Mike hypothesized.

Brydon pursed his lips and scanned the restaurant while TJ kept going on and on. He couldn't see the register from where he was sitting, so any visual confirmation that a Giustina employee had snatched up his card w-

"So long," not-Giustina belted as she tossed Brydon's card and four slips of paper on the table, en route to somewhere more important.

"Wait!"

She skidded to a halt, spun around and lumbered back to Brydon's table. "Whaddyawant?"

Brydon hastily scribbled his name on the receipt and handed it back to her. He muscled up the smile he had last deployed on a spread in *Men's Health*. "You're not gonna keep that for your personal collection, are you?"

Not-Giustina watched him intently. Unbidden, the image of trying to explain a joke to a toad came to Brydon's mind.

"Or sell it?" he pressed on.

"Dude," TJ whispered into his palms.

"'Cuz, you know," Brydon continued, undaunted, "there are definitely people who would pay a lot of money to have me sign their notebooks or their tits or whatever. Like, ten, fifteen bucks."

Not-Giustina scrutinized the receipt. "Well it looks like you just paid seventeen bucks for the honor of givin' me your chickenscratch, how's that?"

"I don't kn-"

Mike put a calming hand on Brydon's arm.

"Dude!"

Mike withdrew his hand.

"I don't know if you like, do you not watch TV? Ever?"

Not-Giustina looked to TJ, to Mike. They looked at her, and then to each other.

Nobody was looking at Brydon.

What the fuck.

"Hey!" he shouted, a bit louder than necessary to get Not-Giustina's attention. A few other grease-faced patrons in the pizzeria turned to look. Noticing the unwanted attention, Brydon throttled back in the hopes of gaining *wanted* attention through persuasion.

"Hey, listen, so I don't know if you know this, but I'm Brydon Plyst."

Once again, Not-Giustina investigated the receipt.

"Sure. Says so here."

Brydon jerked his arms out to the side, a non-verbal *well?* into which the bombshell could sink.

Not-Giustina parried with a verbal "well?"

"Don't you watch TV?"

"Sure."

"And you don't recognize my name? My face?"

"Nah."

Brydon shook his head, incredulous. How was this possible? "*C-C-Craig's Way?*"

"Is that a show?"

"Is that…" he made a *can you believe this?* face at Mike and TJ. They looked like they really could believe it. No help. He turned back to Not-Giustina. "Yes it's a show! And I'm the star!"

"Good for you, sweetie." What infuriated Brydon most about that was that she really sounded earnest in her well-wishing.

Brydon jerked his arms out even further. "So?" A waitress with a pizza nearly clotheslined on his arm.

"Watch it!" she shouted.

"I know, right?" Brydon agreed. "Everybody should be watching it!"

"Kid," Not-Giustina leveled in an uncharacteristic-ally smoky baritone, "I'm real happy for your program, but your receipt's going in the till like any ot-"

"It's not about the receipt," TJ chimed in. "He wants his picture on the wall."

Brydon could barely reply through all of the very real, not fake laughter he was racked by. "Wha-ha-ha-

whaaaAAAAT?"

"You've been staring at them all night, man!"

"Mhm," Mike added.

"I'm just…" Brydon pointed to Rob Lowe's picture. "…who is *that* though?"

"He's a handsome man," Not-Giustina snapped.

"And I'm not?"

"You're a boy, kid."

"I'm a famous boy!"

"I've never heard of you."

"That's not my problem!"

"Well that's something we got in common," Not-Giustina concluded. She bustled off, seeing to her business.

Brydon stared at the space she had been occupying. The view now afforded him a clear view of Mike Meyers smiling next to King Cauliflower. *Mike Myers.*

He folded his arms on the table and hung his head. Any second now, Mike and TJ would be rushing to console him. Any second now.

When no consolation was forthcoming, he lifted his head and snuck a peek.

Mike and TJ were talking to each other about something completely different.

"The fuck, guys?" Brydon wondered as he unfolded his arms.

TJ rolled his eyes and turned back. "Listen, ok, I'm gonna say this as a friend. You don't seem to have any concept of how successful your show is."

Brydon opened his mouth to reply, but Mike

shushed him. The impudence actually stunned him into silence.

"You're on a hit that's only a hit by new-channel standards. But there's a million fucking channels out there. You get on the talk shows and the magazines and everything, and that's cool."

"I'm a bona fide phenomenon," Brydon sulked.

"See but that's where I feel like you're not even listening. You're *not*."

"I'm a millionaire!"

Now it was TJ's turn to be stunned into silence.

Astonishingly, it was Mike who picked up the slack. "I'm gonna go home," he announced as he shuffled out of the booth.

TJ was close behind. "You wanna split a Zyp?"

"Yeah, sure!"

Torn between upbraiding them for bailing and wanting to pay for their ride just so they knew he really *was* a millionaire, Brydon opted to fold his arms and hang his head again.

"Good luck with the show," TJ offered. Mike echoed him a bit more sincerely. And then they were gone.

Brydon stewed in the booth until Not-Giustina told him he had to scram, other customers wanted to sit.

"Please take my picture," he pleaded.

Not-Giustina frowned at him like a toad that finally got the punchline and decided it hadn't been worth the effort. "Kid, I got a business to run."

"And I have a brand to manage! Fucking

appearances!"

"Well how's this, I throw you out on your ass, then we get a picture of you with your head in a puddle. That work for your brand?"

"Pffffft," Brydon blustered as he climbed out of the booth. It was all he could think to say. He couldn't threaten to make sure she'd never work in this town again, he couldn't have his agent call her manager and demand an apology, he couldn't even go on TV and blast her – people either didn't know her, or they loved her. Like Rob Fucking Lowe. "Pffffft," he reiterated on his way out the door.

He called his chauffer then sat down on the curb, his hands in his pockets.

In a few short weeks, cameras would roll on *C-C-Craig's Way* season two. He'd be back in the limelight. Back on top. Making even more fans, more money. Everything would be as it was meant to be. Brydon Plyst, bona fide phenomenon.

A stiff breeze slipped through his coat and rattled his spine. He curled up tighter, chin ducked against the chill. His teeth chattered a little bit. If he tried to speak now, he might well have a real stutter.

He tried it out. "Craig's Way," he muttered. No stutter. He made an effort to help it along. "C-C-Craig." Ok, there was one, but he was trying. "Craig." He loosened his jaw, let it *really* set to chattering, and tried again. "Cr-Craig."

Ok! Not bad. Didn't sound anything like his fake stutter though. His fake stutter was so much better.

He smiled and rocked back and forth on the curb, trying to keep warm until his chauffer came.

Ten minutes later, his phone started buzzing. And buzzing. And buzzing. Figuring it to be his idiot chauffer calling, he pulled out the phone and saw an avalanche of texts from his agent, managers, co-stars and stylists asking if he was alright. They were only asking, he discovered, because a video had just shown up on TMZ of him sitting alone on a curb on a blustery winter night, muttering the word Craig to himself and rocking back and forth.

Five minutes after that, the chauffer called and said he couldn't find where Brydon had said he was on the map. He asked Brydon to find a busier street corner to stand on.

Sighing, Brydon stood up and went trudging off to find one.

why is it a terrible idea to let a baby cook in a five-star restaurant

the steaks are too high

what do you call a pop star who is always saying goodbye

sia

where does a glass of merlot go to get darker

a tannin salon

THERE'S SOMEBODY
IN HERE!

THERE'S SOMEBODY IN HERE!

Nothing compares to the sense of clarity that follows a big, ugly cry. It's what had Suzie feeling so focused since she'd moved to the city with neither friends nor employment awaiting her.

Over the last eleven months, she'd had six big ugly cries, fifteen mid-level cries of the sort where you use a lot of tissues but don't feel it necessary to bring the box over to the couch, and thirty-one of your garden variety 'boo hoo's barely audible over the *thnk* of the spoon hitting the bottom of the Phish Food pint.

The occasion for the move was the messy conclusion of an even messier relationship, one which saw mutual friends taking sides and periodically tagging in to ensure neither Suzie nor Margaret would ever be more than fifteen minutes from some little proxy recrimination. Margaret's response to this was to go on the offensive, waging a literal slash-and-burn war against Suzie and her loyalists (though as far as Suzie was aware, none of her friends had had *their* cherished keepsakes set aflame - so much for solidarity). Suzie's was to cut ties and float off in search of less salted pastures. Her destination was set largely by default, as there was only one major city on the Eastern seaboard where she *didn't* know anybody.

At the time, that had sounded appealing.

Now, on just about the anniversary of her arrival, Suzie was overstressed, overworked, underpaid and undersocialized. She had made some new friends at her job, because where *else* was she going to make them, the subway? Where was she supposed to find enough time to make them at the, the…clubs, or libraries, wherever the hell grown-ass adults go to make friends? Making rent was hard enough. Her 'fun money' amounted to just enough for a 5-piece tender combo from Popeye's (alas, the only real tenderness she had yet found in this city) and a handle of Wild Turkey. It was while partaking of the latter indulgence that she most often fired up Facebook and reconnected with friends from back home. Occasionally she would fish for updates on Margaret; more often, she would talk about other things and hope those details would emerge unsolicited.

These communications almost all occurred via textual mediums, naturally. Suzie hadn't really heard her friends' voices since her departure, save an errant call here or there. She wondered if they got the same charge from seeing her name pop up on their phones and she did to see theirs'. Probably not.

Anyway, yeah, about those friends from work: Suzie punched the clock at a hippie-dippie uptown dance studio called Nong Eye Gong, a cozy two-room space crowning a three-story walkup. The teachers were all *terrific*; Suzie got to take free classes, which was wonderful because memberships typically hit the same price points as Margaret's car payments had, that *bitch*. But what-ever about Margaret. The clientele at Nong Eye Gong were *fine*; for every one that took selfies in front of the class mirrors (invariably stood with their back to the mirror, presumably to get their ass in reflection) and posted them with hashtags like 'Namastepballchange', there was one that had the decency to look at the truly awful merch Nong Eye Gong offered, such as the #namastepballchange tank top, and just walk away. Suzie's coworkers were…*floaty*, that was a sort of nice way to say it. *Clueless* was a bit more pointed, but it hit much closer to the mark. They were almost exclusively white, and appropriated cultures the way most people pile on desserts at a buffet. A hoodie, with a thick golden chain necklace running through a big Devanagari Aum silkscreened onto it? Sure, and why not grab one for yourself for only $74.99? A cheap adhesive Bindi slapped onto the forehead? Of *course*, because doesn't it really just *flow* with my eyeshadow? Temporary, sponge-applied henna tattoos? *Obviously*, though sometimes that's a bit too much work so here's one of the Chinese character for 'water', which is *so* my element.

To be clear, they were all perfectly nice people. Pity they were also perfectly self-centered, only comfortable when discussing the spiritual journeys that they were taking one Deepak Chopra video at a time. Suzie had some genuine affinity for the bohemian aesthetic and mindset, but found it nearly impossible to sustain under such relentless misapplication. Because, ultimately, what if it *wasn't* misapplication? What if this was the apotheosis of *Aum*?

It was this grand reservation (oh, how Suzie hoped nobody came in with a feathered headdress anytime soon) that made it such a challenge to call her fellow Gongers *friends*. They were people to talk to, maybe sometimes (just the one time, really) go out for drinks with. But to call *friends*, with all of the stripping of pose and pretense that implies? Impossible. Strip these people of their pretense and all you'd have left would be a skeleton throwing spiritual gang symbols.

So no friends, then. Eleven months and no friends. Two jobs, both of which she still worked. And, lest we forget, six moments of vivid clarity.

"I think when I go home, I'm gonna write a blog post about, like, paleo. Not enough people are talking about paleo anymore."

Suzie stopped typing, looked up from the guest list and smiled at Trixie, her supervisor. "Oh yeah?" That, Suzie had long since discovered, was the safest way to reply to her coworkers when they said something that sounded like, but was not, the beginning of an actual human conversation. It was a prompt for them to commence the monologue, in the hopes they would tire themselves out and fall asleep.

"Yeah," Trixie continued as Suzie resumed copying the guest list into the system. "Because I really think that, like, I've discovered that I feel so much more, I don't know, I just feel like if everybody else ate healthier, like don't just eat whatever gets put in front of you, but shop local and buy local and then not only are your, not only is your produce more healthy and greener but it's also, you can *trust* it because it's local, and if people would just focus more on that because also because it's going to really change the environment and I think not enough people are talking about that either, like we can really, like, we can make a difference for the planet and we can even, like, save the *world* and all we have to do is be a bit more mindful of our bodies and the food we're putting into them, and the vibes we're giving out because, you know that like I'm an empath, so I can really just tell what somebody is giving and so I know that when I'm giving it and they're *receiving* a more mindful embodiment, which can also really turn things around because I think politically we're all more than ever because we're not giving out the right things and we're also not receiving the right things, like if there was just a way to really feel what people want instead of asking them because that's how you get a President like we have, *ugh*, and I think like I once said in my blog last week, I really went *off* on Trump and I did not hold back, I told it like it was and I'm not even worried if he hears it, really I hope he does, but that's partly why I really want to focus on something positive because there was honestly like a lot of negativity in that post and I'm not a negative person, I'm so positive, like, you know, so this post I'm working on that I'm going to write tonight is probably going to be about how important it is to be just like *aware* because so many people aren't, I see so many people who aren't even thinking about the things they're doing or saying or the impact those things have on other people and I'm like hell-O wake up, there's only ti-"

Dora, one of the dance instructors, glided out of the locker room with a duffel bag strap and a scarf competing for clavicle real estate. "Have a great night!" she suggested.

"You too!" Suzie called enviously. Just a few more guests to log and then she, too, was out the door.

"Peaceful dreams!" Trixie bade Dora. "As I was saying, my blog. I was talking about…what was I saying?"

"Done!" Suzie announced a bit too eagerly. She spun her chair towards Trixie. "What do you say we get outta here, you can get cracking on that post?"

"Oh my god," Trixie replied, "that sounds *so* chill."

And on that, they could both agree.

"You go on ahead," Suzie insisted for the fourth time. "I've gotta tidy up."

Trixie, bundled up in her marshmallow parka, didn't budge from her spot right next to the door. "No no no, I can *so* wait for you. We can walk to the train together!"

The walk to the train was four sketchy blocks through an industrial part of town. Suzie was often taking it at 11:30 P.M., as she would be tonight. It was a genuinely frightening walk, but if the options were 'walk with Trixie' and 'walk alone', she would stick a hand in her pocket, push her keys between her fingers like Wolverine and take her chances.

Still, Trixie's desperation for company likely stemmed from that common fear, one of the few things they had in common, as much as it did from her insatiable need to be heard and validated. Suzie felt for the girl, but she wasn't a *martyr*. Trixie could just blog-post monologue her way to the train, and any ne'er-do-wells would give her a very wide berth.

"I'm actually not gonna take the train," Suzie fibbed. Fibbing wasn't her style, but nothing in Nong Eye Gong could be mistaken for *anybody's* style, so she figured it was alright.

"Oh?"

Suzie almost stood, but that would have perhaps signaled something she had no intention of signaling. Trixie couldn't read signals, but she could sure as hell write them into other people's behavior. So Suzie slumped even further into her seat, which seemed safe. "Yeah, I'm gonna…my girlfriend is picking me up."

"Ooooh, you've got a girlfriend?"

It was a stab in the heart to realize that, as that lie had escaped Suzie's mouth, she'd genuinely forgotten that she *didn't* have one anymore. Margaret had burrowed in deep, and even a year removed Suzie was still pulling weeds. This was something to think about, but not now because Trixie was closing in for a probing conversation that would inevitably circle around to the time she kissed a girl when she was drunk at a party and that would go spiraling off into the night before boomeranging back to the podcast she was threatening to start so Suzie quickly said "yep, yeah but she's not gonna be here for a while so you should just go on ahead."

Trixie halted her approach. Her face fell. "Aw, alright. Well, have fun!" And then she turned, slipped out the door and became vanishing footfalls echoing in the stairwell. And then the door closed, and Suzie was alone.

A great weight lifted from her shoulders. Sure, she felt a little bit bad about consigning Trixie to the frosty dark alone. But only a little bit.

She leaned back in her chair, savoring the timid *squeak* and the ancient *creak* it made, how each was gobbled up by greedy silence. And what a lovely hush it was; quiet was something nearly impossible to find in the city, especially at Nong Eye Gong, where people were either dancing, singing or Trixie.

But sometimes, late at night, when she had the place to herself, Suzie found silence here in the studio. And with it, a dusty smile.

As last employee out, it was proper procedure to give the studio a once-over. Not that it took much work; peek into Room 1, check that it's empty and the lights are out, try not to imagine coming upon a lone figure standing in the center of the room, a long-limbed silhouette against the window, slowly turning turning

turning to face you, a cackle rising in its throat…peek into Room 2 and repeat, then head to the break 'room', i.e. the closet into which somebody had tossed a folding chair, and poke into the restroom nested within.

All empty, all the lights off. Suzie navigated by the nervous neon sign just outside the window, which never stopped humming about the nail salon on the second floor even after all the ladies had called it a day. She wondered if it knew.

She shut down the relic of a desktop behind the front desk and double-checked that the cash drawer was locked. Running a hand along the desk to stay oriented (the NAILS sign provided a dim crimson by which to steer, but it also threw heavy shadows), Suzie stepped around towards the door and clipped a rack of messenger bags scarred with the words "GLITTER QUEEN" for some fucking reason. A pointy bit popped her hard in the kidney.

"*Oof.*" Her hands flew to the offended area at once. Remarkably, the pain ebbed.

What remained was another sensation.

Suzie looked at her phone. 12:04 A.M. She looked up at the break 'room' door. It was a fifty minute train ride home, and at this hour the F trains only showed up once every fifteen minutes or so. If that. She might not be home for over an hour.

F *that*.

Moving slowly through the strawberry nightmare, Suzie stumbled into the break 'room'. She closed the door behind her, because the quarters were too cramped to have the break room door *and* the bathroom doors open at once. Ordinarily, this meant that if Suzie or another employee was on their break, and a customer needed to take a shit, there would follow the sort of theatrical, frowning shuffle that has made many a window-seat flier blush. At times like *these*, when the room was empty, it was merely a minor annoyance.

Suzie clicked on the bathroom light, shut the door, dropped trough and plopped down. The waterworks began at once. Ah, that was better. She had really had to pee, it seemed. Maybe bumping that stupid rack saved her s-

Knock knock knock. A polite rap on the door.

"There's somebody in here!" Suzie replied as she threaded out a few squares of toilet pap…

…

No, there wasn't. There was nobody here. She'd checked.

A final runlet of pee splashed into the bowl.

"Trixie? Did you forget something?"

…

Knock, knock, knock.

She hadn't heard the door to the break 'room' open. That could only mean it *hadn't* opened – the hinges were too squeaky, the construction of this little cubby too poor.

But there was absolutely no way somebody could have been hiding in the break 'room' as she passed through. There was nowhere *to* hide.

As quietly as she could, Suzie tugged the toilet paper

off the roll, balled it up and saw to a less terrifying situation. She fancied she'd feel a lot better about this with her pants on.

She reached below herself. Her knuckles splashed into the water. She had never trembled like this. It was like cold electrocution.

There was no way out of the bathroom, except through that door. And what a bathroom it was, maybe two feet wide and five feet long, toilet at one end, sink at the other. You could just about pee and wash your hands at the same time. No windows. No human-sized vents to crawl through.

"Is somebody there?"

. . .

. . .

. . .

Suzie checked her phone. Great service. All she had to do was call 911, lay out the situation, and wait.

But the door to the break 'room' hadn't opened. If it had, she'd feel confident that there was some regular old bad guy on the other side of this door, a classic bastard with a face perfect for throwing books at. Without the telltale complaints of that other door, though...Suzie could only think of two op-

Knock. Knock. Knock.

A reedy groan escape her. There were two things that could cause disembodied knocking. The first was something spooky. Enough spirituality lingered within her to make this worth considering, but she'd never really believed in *ghosts*. There was a difference, one she'd never articulated but one she nevertheless embraced. Something spooky, that was option one.

The second was that she was losing her mind.

Hardly implausible. A year of constant anxiety with no real release, th-

KNOCK. KNOCK. KNO-

"JUST A SECOND!" she screamed reflexively. Her hands, always eager and never early, clapped themselves over her mouth.

No reaction from the other side of the door.

Suzie wasn't prepared to say that there was an 'it' to make angry, but nor was she prepared to say that there *wasn't*.

She stared at the doorknob, which as yet had not jiggled menacingly.

Her eyes nearly fell out of her head.

The door was unlocked.

She poked the little button on the knob. *Click.* Now it was locked.

Teeth clenched, Suzie wrestled with the fact that not all doors are created equal. This particular specimen was so thin and poorly set, you could cut it in half with a mean-spirited comment and slide it underneath itself.

And it had been unlocked.

If there really was something out there, and it really wanted to get in *here*, then it would have already. It was just that simple.

So what, then? If it didn't want to come *in*, then it must want her to go *out*.

Or she was just losing her mind.

THERE'S SOMEBODY IN HERE!

She imagined calling 911, imagined blubbering her situation into the phone, but couldn't imagine any version of a 'rescue' that didn't end with her running from men with butterfly nets.

For a change of pace, Suzie stopped considering the causes and started mulling over solutions. She had three next steps; wait here an indefinite amount of time, call 911, or open the door. That was it. Those were the three things.

She didn't want to just sit in here for no reason. She didn't want to call 911 screaming about being afraid to leave the bathroom of a dance studio where she worked. She also didn't want to open the door. But she didn't want to open the door *less* than she didn't want to do those two other things.

All that could stop her now was taking a moment to think about it. She wrapped her hand around the knob, twisted and shoved.

Two things happened at once: first, the door hit something where there should have been nothing. Suzie screamed, though the obstruction itself was nearly silent. It felt, and sounded, like she's swung the door into the overstuffed beanbag chair. The door slammed itself shut, *hard*.

Second, she remembered that she had been, and was now again, sitting on an unflushed toilet with her pants around her ankles.

THUM THUM THUM THUM, an open palm thundered against the door, shaking it in the frame.

Suzie screamed as she carefully bent down and lifted

up her pants.

THUM THUM THUM THUM

She continued to scream as she zipped the fly and cinched her belt.

THUM THUM THUM THUM

She stopped screaming when she flushed the toilet, because it is physically impossible for a human to scream in terror while flushing a toilet.

"STOP IT!" she cried, once the pisswater had swirled out of sight. "JUST LEAVE ME ALONE!"

THUM THUM THUM THUM

Wailing something that certainly wasn't language, Suzie whapped the door with her own open palm. The right hand smarted, and the left rushed to console. But Suzie tore them apart and redoubled her onslaught. "I JUST WANNA FUCKING GO HOME!"

THUM THUM THUM THUM

She pounded on the door until her palms were raw, then she balled them into fists and hit twice as hard.

THUM THUM THUM THUM

War cries bounced around the tall casket of the bathroom like most of the checks Suzie had ever written. Was the thing on the other side of the door screaming too?

THUM THUM THUM THUM

It wasn't until tears unspooled themselves on her cheeks that she realized she was crying. It was a big, ugly cry, the seventh of the year. Lucky number seven, in the bathroom of Nong Eye Gong.

Suzie sobbed and snarled and pounded and kicked,

for how long it was impossible to say.

And then, like a cloud, it passed.

All at once, she stopped, letting her hands fall to her sides. Panting, sweating, weeping, Suzie listened to her heartbeat ticking down, down, down into something approaching manageable.

KnockknockKnockknockKnockknock. The thing on the other side of the door tapped along to Suzie's heart.

Was that the sort of thing a crazy person would imagine? She no longer doubted her sanity; she just straight up didn't trust that motherfucker. What kind of a woman goes beast mode on a bathroom door unless she's got more than a few brown bananas in her bunch? Still, brown bananas are good for banana bread. Yes, that is true.

Crying makes for clarity, but nobody said anything about coherence.

It was entirely possible that she was imagining this entire episode. That it was some externalization of her anxiety. Loads of people had nervous breakdowns – why not her?

Knockknock, Knockknock, Knockknock.

She couldn't decide which possibility troubled her more – that she was hallucinating, or that she *wasn't*.

Well, assuming she survived the night, why not get a second opinion?

Suzie pulled her phone back out and blipped on the flashlight. It pinned the sink in its glare, the intensity of which never failed to astonish her. Little gems of water swelled on the rim of the faucet and dripped into the porcelain below.

They were dripping in time to the knocking of the door. And so, her heart.

All three got just a little bit faster.

KnockknockKnockknockKnockknock.

Suzie shook the willies away. Pure distraction. She had a job to do.

She got down on her hands and knees, bowing to the god of indoor plumbing as she pressed her temple onto the cold linoleum. There was nothing to see under the door, of course. She hadn't turned the lights on out there.

An urge to kick herself was quickly chased away by the self-confidence Suzie often forgot she had, and frankly the self-confidence would have preferred it that way. Frustrated at being aroused, it groused, How could you possibly have anticipated this? and returned to a liminal doze.

Suzie had no reply.

Instead, she brought her phone just below her eyes, the unflinching iOfSauron illuminating all of the break 'room', up to a height of about one inch. No feet standing just outside the door. The knocking continued, faster still to keep pace with the conductor.

KnkknkKnkknkKnk

She pulled up camera mode on her phone. Switched to video.

Ah, Hell. She'd wanted to slide the phone under the door and watch the screen, to glimpse the other side in real time. But the light was on the back of the phone.

She'd have to put it screen-down on the ground, slide it under the door, and then just watch the video when she pulled it back. It came out to acquiring the same information just a few seconds later than she'd wanted…assuming the thing didn't just rip the door off its hinges and *knock knock* her eyes out the back of her head.

Which it could have done already, if it had wanted to. Unless it was just toying with her.

Unless, also, she was just batshit bonkers.

Just to be safe, she poked the little button on the knob again. *Click*. Safe and sound again, ha, ha.

She placed the phone screen-down on the ground.

NknkNknkNknk, the thing must have been using two hands to knock that fast. If it used hands at all.

Suzie slid the phone under the door. The light that had been filling the bathroom vanished beneath the edge. Hopefully illu-

"Oh, fuck!" she cried. She'd forgotten to hit record!

She slid the phone, which was by that point almost entirely in the break 'room', back into the bathroom. Tried to, anyway. It held firm, as though glued to the ground.

Suzie shifted her position for a better grip. The phone slipped out of her hand, zipping the rest of the way under the door. As if yanked.

And yet, the knocking never ceased. It kept such perfect time.

So that was a point for *not crazy*, right? She had not only seen it but *felt* it yanked from beneath her fingers.

Not that a crazy person *couldn't* imagine those things, but, well, it was probably harder. Right? Tactile hallucination, that was probably Advanced Screwball material. Suzie had only just begun auditing Bugnuts 101.

Or maybe she was just an overachiever.

The knocking stopped. The sink kept dripping, though to be fair that had been a problem at Nong Eye Gong for a lot longer than ghost knocking.

Suzie's phone slipped back under the door, screen-up.

On the screen was a picture of something Suzie couldn't make out.

She picked the phone up, eager for a closer look but hesitant to bring it too close to her face.

Her heartbeat ticked up, up, up, but the knocking let her take the solo. Even the leaky faucet ducked out. It was just Suzie's heart, traitorous silence, and the picture on the phone.

She stared at it for two straight minutes, mute and motionless. She wouldn't give this thing the satisfaction of a reaction. Even though it had already given *her* something.

Proof.

She texted the picture to Dawn, who had stuck by Suzie most tenaciously at the height of Margaregeddon. Dawn was just about the only person who would believe Suzie *wasn't* fucking with them.

The three little dots that announced the composition of a response failed to materialize. But the message and image had been delivered, s-

Suzie's phone rang. Dawn.

She answered. "Dawn!"

"What the fuck?"

Suzie's brow fell like Dorothy's house. She looked at her phone, which happily reported that she was now Connected With Margaret.

The house had missed, apparently.

"I…" Suzie put the phone on speaker as she pulled up her texts again.

There it was – the picture, sent to Margaret. Dawn didn't enter into it at all.

So that was a point for team *crazy*.

Suzie took the phone off speaker. "I'm really sorry Margaret, it's a long story but I'm kind of in trouble and I need you to tell me what you see in the picture I just sent you."

"Have you been crying?" Margaret asked it the way people point to a pile of shit on the heirloom rug and ask their dog, 'did you do this?'

"Yes," Suzie replied. No time to posture.

The *thing* outside the door tapped the frame impatiently.

Suzie *thump*ed the door hard with her fist.

"You've got a lot of nerve," Margaret wound up.

Unable to help it, Suzie swung before the pitch. "Oh, here we go."

She heard a gasp on the other end of the line. It sounded like it had been pressed through a smile. "Honestly, for a second I thought this was some dipshit way of apologizing. But no, yo-"

"MARGARET! What's in the picture?!"

"Whatever game you th-"

"Can you not see it?!"

"Of course I can fucking see it!"

"So? What is it?"

"It's your fucking...doll, your rabbit doll thing!"

"Which you told me you burned!"

"I did! Are you still pi-"

"*Then what is Hop doing in Nong Eye Gong?!*"

"...is that in Vietnam?"

Suzie hung up. She'd gotten all she needed. A beloved stuffed animal from her childhood, which she had retained into adulthood for sentimental reasons, and which Margaret had just reiterated she did, in fact, burn one of the many times Suzie sought shelter at Dawn's house...was sitting on the table in the break 'room' of Nong Eye Gong. Staring straight down the barrel of the camera, washed out in that unflattering phone flash.

The picture had been taken from about the height of Suzie's belly button. And that, on top of everything else, was inexplicably what convinced her.

This was happening. It wasn't a delusion. That was proof. Occam's razor was now cutting the other way: was it more likely that she had purchased a brand new Hop, artificially aged and distressed it to match *exactly* the Hop she'd known prior to its immolation, placed it on the table, taken the photo at *belly button height* (come *on*), and then constructed a fantasy in which none of that had ever happened and she was trapped in the bathroom with the image on her phone, timestamped at *precisely* the time she had fabricated the sight of it being returned to her after being taken...*or*, was she actually trapped in the bathroom because some half-squat specter capable of snatching items from her past and placing them on t-

Ok, the second one was still sounding crazier than she'd have liked.

On the other hand, *belly button height.*

Therefore: This was happening.

No question.

Except, question: now what?

It was trying to tell her something. The doll, the redirected text to Margaret (which had to have happened, Suzie was *positive* she'd sent the picture to Dawn)... what was it trying to say?

"Listen..." she said, and she imagined she could *hear* it listening. It was a sound with scales. "I want to know what *you* want. Just...do you talk?"

...nothing.

"Knock once for yes and twice for no. Do you understand?"

Knock knock.

"Um..." Suzie looked down at the picture on her phone. There was Hop, plopped on the folding chair, watching her sweat...

In situations like these, there were no dumb questions.

"Will Hop talk to me?"

That scaly sound again.

"Why are you doing this?"

Scales.

"What did I ever do to you, huh? Did I do something wrong?"

Nothing.

"I'm sick of this shit!" Suzie reached for the knob, twisted and pushed. As before, the door opened a crack, hit something, and slammed shut again.

As before, the banging.

THUM THUM THUM THUM

"I'm not even scared of you anymore!" Which was almost the truth.

THUM THUM THUM THUM

"Keep banging asshole, laugh it up!" She kicked the door. "I have to get up at six in the fucking A.M. to go work my *other* job, because I have to work two jobs just to live in this piece of shit city I don't even like! It smells like shit and everybody is here an asshole and I'm gonna be exhausted if I ever *get* to my *second job*, because I have to deal with whatever the fuck *your* problem is!" A few more kicks.

THUM THUM THUM THUM

"Do you even have a fucking clue how hard I have to work, *without* getting locked in the bathroom by some sex pervert ghost who likes to spook women while they're peeing? Do you pay rent? What the hell do you know? Who even asked you?"

THUM THUM THUM THUM

"I bet you have a million fucking ghost friends, you're fucking with me so you can go tell them how bad you pranked me, like ha ha were you watching on your ghost TV or some shit like that, did you see her face, you and your billion fucking ghost friends, well guess what, whatever man! *FUCK YOU.*"

THUM THUM THUM THUM

"WHY DON'T YOU GO PISS, YOU SHIT, SEE HOW IT FEELS?"

Suzie slammed her knuckles into the door, intending to knock ironically, or at least see if such a thing were possible.

She got as far as *knock knock knock.*

The banging stopped. The door popped open and creaked a few inches out into the break 'room'.

Silence.

She pushed the door the rest of the way open. It wheedled and whined, but did as it was bidden. There were no obstructions.

There was, however, something to see by the expanding light of the bathroom.

Hop.

Without a doubt, *the* Hop. Suzie would know that rabbit anywhere. Even here, now.

She stepped forward, closing the bathroom door behind her. The overstressed 40w bulb wasn't willing to follow her through, but her phone's stargasm eyefucker was *beyond* excited to take over.

Unmistakably Hop. Suzie crouched down, ran the phonelight around it like a Geiger counter. No beeps or beats or knocks. Just Hop.

Could she take it home? Was it a booby prize, for

toilet time served? The idea had a mysterious appeal. It would have been a stupendously dumb thing to do, accepting something that was almost *certainly* haunted.

And yet...

This was a chance to have something back. Something Margaret had taken from her. A piece of the past, from way back when she really only cried from laughing too hard.

All she had to do was reach out and take it.

Her hand crept towards Hop, as always acting of its own volition. Dead steady, she noted. Neither tremor nor tremble.

She halted the hand. Perhaps it was a lingering sense of clarity, or perhaps Hop was decaying before her eyes. Either way, blights and imperfections on the doll each made claims on her attention; a split seam here, a wisp of cotton there. None of these were *new*, of course. They were a part of Hop's character. Which was a cute way of saying the rabbit looked like it had chewed on a few too many funny carrots. She'd been able to ignore or contextualize the bruises when Hop had been *there*, a part of the furniture as reliable as the bed upon which it lay. But a little distance brought it, ha ha, home:

Hop had seen better days. But that didn't necessarily mean Hop's days were better.

Suzie left Hop right where it was and squeezed through the door into a red festival of kitsch. The tireless white of her phone carved her a path to the door.

THERE'S SOMEBODY IN HERE!

It took her two and a half hours to get home. And all that time, she was *clear*. It was rare that the psychic burlap was lifted from her eyes for such a long period of time, but that last cry had been a *really* good one, apparently.

The walk to the train was as sketchy as she'd always remembered. And yet, even in the rather pathetic tents of vision thrown by unevenly spaced streetlights, Suzie saw things she had never really noticed before. Or, maybe that wasn't right. It *definitely* wasn't. It was just… she saw things she had seen a million times, just a bit more clearly.

That was it. That was closer to it, anyway.

Her breath wriggled through her scarf and puffed upwards.

Old snow still had enough crunch left in it to cheer her passage.

Her fingers tingled in her pockets, and they would tingle again once they were warm.

She would go to bed, and then have to get up two hours after that. But now wasn't the time to think about that. Plenty of time to wallow in her misfortunes, when she was feeling more muddled.

Tonight was clear. And quiet.

By the time she got back to her building, the shiny bits of the night had gone dull again. Her feet were tired, the train had been unsettling. But once or twice on the walk home she thought she'd spotted snow-flakes, which was cause for keeping the spirits up.

Maybe there'd be a snow day. Nobody has to go to work. Especially not her.

Should she just call in sick?

Too late for that, they'd assume she'd be-

Tomorrow. Set the alarm and worry about it tomorrow. Er, later today.

Suzie clomped her boots against the side of the porch stairs, pounding off as much of the snow as she could. Hands in her pockets, head retracted into the scarf, she turtled up the stairs. After a bit of fumbling, she keyed her way through both doors and harrumphed up another flight to her apartment. She pulled her key out, held it in front of her and jousted her door.

Her aim was true, the key plunging straight into the lock.

Knock knock knock.

Suzie stared at the lock, slowly lifting her gaze to the center of her door. Right about the spot somebody had knocked on it.

From inside her apartment.

She tried the knob without turning the key. It was still locked.

There was terror, yes, but also annoyance. She'd been *through* this already.

Knock, knock, knock.

And anger.

Frustration, fury and fear. The three F's. She could think of a fourth. Well, five, if you counted 'fourth'. 'Five' made six.

Fuck.

What about another? Why not make it seven, her lucky fucking number?

Suzie felt, there, that was seven. Suzie felt some ugly things, but she wouldn't always. They would pass, eventually. Like a fucking fever.

Fuck, fever made eight, didn't it? Was that progress?

She closed her eyes and breathed through her nose. Yes, she had been through this already.

Which meant she could probably get through it again, if she had to.

She lifted her hand, curled into a loose fist with the bent first finger poking out a bit further than the rest, and placed her knuckle against the cool wood between her and whatever was on the other side.

She knocked on her own door like she owned it.

Knock. Knock. Knock.

how did the head of the catholic church get caught
embezzling

he left a papal trail

what do you call it when your doctor tells you to pause
as you're describing your symptoms

a medically induced comma

what website do millions of people use to find out
which of their family members have slept together

incestry.com

WINNER WINNER

1

All the guys in suits seemed nervous, but Pally didn't see why. They weren't the ones signing just about every page of a three-inch paper stack.

"And here," the guy called Reginald indicated, quite redundantly. The lines requiring Pally's signature were tagged with post-its, and highlighted in yellow just in case that weren't enough. Like they thought he was an idiot or something! "And here."

Pally was too giddy to take it personally. He probably *was* acting sort of idiot…ly. Idiotish. Stupid. How could he not, though? He had won big, bigger than he'd ever won in his life. Granted, he wasn't the kind of guy whose biography was riddled with wins in the first place, but this was the sort of victory that balanced the cosmic scales, atoned for Pally's heretofore rotten luck.

A lifetime supply of gas from Tort-Oil, for him and his family, won in a contest he'd entered for free online. His being a two car household (going on three, once that far-off day when Lily came of driving age finally arrived) just outside of Los Angeles, removing gas from the annual expenses would save the Hollen family tens of thousands of dollars per year, at *least*. Five figures of income suddenly freed up for vaca-tions and gadgets and yeah alright Lily's college fund, but you can't spell fund with *fun*, which Pally didn't take for an accident.

With each flip of the page, each stroke of the pen, Pally's eagerness redoubled. As soon as he left here, he was planning on driving north on the 101, past Thou-sand Oaks and Camarillo, as far north as he could get on a single tank. Once the needle dipped into the red, he'd pull into the first Tort-Oil station he found, maybe even wave at their big dumb turtle mascot Myrtle, fill that empty tank up up up, for free free *free*, and drive home. All without spending a red cent, or green dollar, or whatever color credit was.

So why were the suits all so nervous? And why were there so many of them? The window-walled board room consisted of one long table, Pally having been granted the head furthest from the door, and at least eight old white guys in high-shouldered suits frowning by turns at Pally and each other.

"Here," Reginald insisted. "And here."

Pally couldn't help but notice a growing mumble from a far clutch of suits, nor the glacial pace at which the youngest of them (and also the only dress) broke off and drifted towards the dwindling stack of papers to be signed. Gently, she placed a finger on the page Pally was just prepared to autograph, right on the yum-yum yellow spot for which his pen was destined.

"Hello Mr. Hollen," the young gun cooed, "may I call you Patrick?"

"You can call me Pally," Patrick Hollen replied, his gaze flitting between this new face and the yellow place. "That's what my friends call me, and anybody who gives me a prize is a friend of mine!"

"Mhm. Well Pally, my name is Julia Berman, head of PR."

"Head of PR, is that a family name? Ha, ha!"

Julia smiled wanly. "Now, forgive me, but it's just this *bonhomie* of yours that I find slightly concerning. My colleagues are satisfied that you're signing these papers fully cognizant of their contents, but I can see, again, forgive me for making an assumption, but it really doesn't appear as though you're reviewing the documents prior to signing them."

Pally shrugged. "They're highlighted so I don't have to."

"Berman," boomed a voice from the huddle that had shed Julia. "It's fine."

Julia sighed and leaned over, nearly resting her entire forearms on the pages now. "Perhaps I should amend my previous statement: my colleagues are satisfied that you're signing these papers, *period*. My concern is that you're not wholly grasping what it is you're agreeing to."

"A lifetime supply of gas," Pally informed her, defensiveness creeping in to his tone.

"Yes," Julia nodded. "That's correct. But is that all you think you're assenting to, by affixing your signature to these documents?"

Pally stared at Julia. Where the hell was she going with this?

"Did you read the fine print at all? Or any of the print?"

Pally rolled his eyes. "What, am I not supposed to tell anybody I won the free gas or something?"

Julia's face grew harder. "Did you watch the video on the website prior to entering the contest?"

An empty spot opened up in Pally's gut. This kid was starting to make him nervous. "What are you driving at? Ha," he added. "Driving! I didn't even do that on pur-"

"*Pally*," Julia snapped. "For God's sake, stop signing and have a lawyer review these with you!"

"*Berman!*" boomed the voice again.

Julia spun on her heels and charged at a group of men who were undoubtedly her superiors, her pointer finger leading the way. The kid had balls, then. Not literally. Well, Pally couldn't say for sure, and upon further consideration, Julia's hardware was irrelevant; it was her software Pally was admiring.

"You don't see the blowback potential on this?" she demanded.

"Out," the biggest, baldest suit ordered.

"How do we spin it when it gets out, our contest winner didn't underst-"

"*Out.*"

"I'm doing my job!"

"If you want it to remain your job, then leave this

goddamned room right this instant!"

Julia, now nearly nose-to-nose with her boss, looked ready to bite his beak clean off. When she spun on her heels to face Pally, the fury etched into her face so startled him that he nearly tipped over backwards in his chair.

"You're signing your life away," she told him with a chillingly flat affect. "Rev-"

"*BERMAN! OUT!*"

Shaking her head, Berman went out. Then it was just Pally, the suits, and the papers.

Reginald cleared his throat, apologized for the disruption, and told Pally to sign *here* and *here*, and once more *here*.

"What did she mean?" Pally asked him, "What was she so worked up about?"

The booming voice from the other end of the room grew a body and rumbled its way to Pally's side, placing a meaty hand on his shoulder. "You know how women get," it growled, "when they're on the rag."

Pally found the comment distasteful, but all at once he realized he didn't know the name of the man whose rockslab palm was bearing down on his shoulder. All he knew was that he was the kind of man who could order people out of rooms. He felt suddenly, indefinably unnerved by the situation.

"Would you mind," Pally ventured, "if I did have somebody look this over and explain this to me?"

"Heeeey," the man croaked in an apparent attempt at camaraderie, "don't let Berman get into your head.

You watched the video on the website, right?"

"Um." Pally had not, as a matter of fact, watched the video. He'd been kind of tipsy, tending towards drunk when he entered the contest. LIFETIME SUPPLY OF GAS FROM TORT-OIL had been sufficiently enticing to him, and besides, the thumbnail of that video was Myrtle the Turtle in his traditional, hailing-a-cab-and-thrilled-about-it pose. Pally hadn't had any interest in some promo video with a nattering cartoon character trying to make petroleum and economics *fun*. "I'm gonna be honest with you, I did not watch the video."

"Aw, come on," sighed a mop-haired kid in the corner, who Pally intuited was probably in charge of whatever department made those stupid little videos nobody watched.

Pally turned back to the nameless bossman to ask if he'd missed anything by skipping the video, but the big guy wasn't looking at Pally anymore. He was looking at Reginald, who was looking at the ceiling like he was hearing footsteps from upstairs when *nobody had lived there for X number of years*. The horror concluded, Reginald lowered his gaze to The Boss and shrugged.

At this, The Boss smiled down on Pally, giving him one last slap on the back. "Nothing much," he beamed. "Say, have you ever eaten at Turelli's? Of course not, it's impossible to get in. I happen to know the chef. He's quite good. I can get you a table, easy as pie. Soon as we're all signed up here, I'll get on the phone, as getting you a table is as simple as picking up the phone. For me."

"Oh neat," Pally said, "what kind of food do they make?"

This was, apparently, the wrong question.

"Here," Reginald continued, "and here."

And because Pally was as good as his name, a sobriquet which had derived from his hopelessly deep-seated need to please, he signed there and there.

2

That whole awkward contract-signing behind him, Pally was eager to give the free gas card its inaugural swipe. He chugged north along the 101 just like he'd planned, even made it to the Pacific Coast Highway before he'd needed to gas up. Unfortunately, there hadn't been any overly friendly, human-toothed turtles staining the horizon, so Pally had to pull in to some dumb old Shell (which could *also* have had a turtle as a mascot, they definitely missed a trick on that one) and pay for gas like a schmuck. Savvy schmuck that he was, he only filled the tank halfway, then looked up the nearest Tort-Oil station on his phone. It was further north along the coast, which would be quite a ways out of the way, so he found one further off that was on his intended route of return. Unfortunately again, he hit rush hour traffic heading back, which never ceased to amaze him, why were people heading *towards* the city at the end of a work day, did that mean they lived *in* the city, one of the most expensive in the country, but commuted to work *outside* of it? What madness was that? It was baffling on a good day but enraging today, as the stop-and-go gridlock sucked up all six gallons in the tank like a young Pally succumbing to peer pressure. So he'd had to pull off and stop *again* at a non Tort-Oil station. This time he elected to pull off the highway, give himself a quarter-tank, then grab dinner somewhere and wait for the crush to subside. In a few hours, it would be smooth sailing to that Tort-Oil station just south of Ventura.

Directly across from the Sunoco station at which Pally got his not-so-top up teetered a kitschy chrome-crusted diner. It was postcard-perfect, complete with the neon lights and, he could see through the massive windows, tabletop jukeboxes.

Pally had always loved diner food, and besides, he and Katie had reservations at that restaurant he'd forgotten the name of that the guy whose name he'd never learned had made for him for the following night. It would be a funny contrast, to eat at the diner one night and…the fancy place the next.

He crossed the street wondering who he could call to figure out what that dang restaurant was called.

Katie picked up on the third ring, which at this hour probably meant she was busy with Lily. "Hey!" she chirped. "How did it go?"

Pally had been thinking long and hard about which very funny joke he would deploy on this phone call. After much careful deliberation, he'd settled on "better stock up on Gas-X babe, because we've got a *lifetime supply*! Of gas," he clarified, because he only now realized the phrasing he went with could be interpreted as his having won a lifetime supply of Gas-X. Rats!

Katie groaned into the phone, which was precisely the reaction Pally had been hoping for. They both laughed as Pally walked past the SEAT YOURSELF sign and headed for a booth by the window in back.

"How far up did you get?" she asked him.

"Up a ways on the PCH! Heading back now but the traffic is out of control. I'm stopping off for some grub, gonna let it die down a bit. Is that ok?"

He heard Katie and Lily talking to each other away from the phone. It was Lily's voice that took control of the conversation: "Daddy?"

"Hi!" Pally settled in to the delightfully uncomfortable dry-wipe fabric of indefinable provenance that cushioned every self-respecting diner's furniture. "How was school?"

"Dumb. We're doing division."

Pally smiled. "Learning that stuff is no fun, but you have to do it."

"How come?"

Sigh. This was the point in the conversation where Pally invariably felt like a fraud. He'd gone to college and done alright, but now made his bacon running cables on mid-level film sets. It was hard, fun work, and there was certainly a fair amount of know-how that went into regulating how much electricity was being used, or the most spatially efficient way to thread the wires. But it wasn't as though he was an Oxford don, and Pally dreaded the day when his daughter's nebulous 'how come's became more focused on 'well, *you* don't use it's. He shuddered to imagine Lily going through a late-teen contrarian streak just as she was getting in to calculus, like a blood moon eclipsing a dying sun.

For now, though, Pally could just say "you'll need it, in life." Lily had inherited enough of her father's agreeability, and her mother's intuitive brilliance, to recognize that any pressing of this particular point would only send the conversation into less amiable climes.

"Ok," Lily agreed. "When are you g-"

His daughter's voice sank into a sea of popping, shuffling noises.

Pally looked at his phone – the call was still connected – and returned it to his ear. "Hello?"

"Patrick," Katie whispered into the phone. Full name. Another blood moon rising. "Why didn't you tell me?"

"Tell you what?"

"Take your order?"

Pally looked up to the waitress who had come slinking out of the shadows to take his order. "Sorry?"

"'Sorry'?!" Katie hissed over the phone.

"Sorry," he told her, "not you."

"Take your order?" the waitress repeated.

"In a minute," he told her. To the phone he said "sorry about that."

The waitress planted a fist on the table. "You gotta order somethin if you wanna sit, mister."

"Sorry," he told her. "Just a beer for now then, I'll look at the menu."

"You're *drinking* right now?" the phone shouted with Katie's voice.

"I have to order something," he explained.

"Why didn't you tell me?" she repeated.

"What kinda beer you want?" the waitress asked.

Pally dropped the phone from his ear and shook his head at the waitress, whose nametag insisted she was called Ann. "Any, Ann. Any beer."

"We got Bud Light," she began.

"Sounds good."

"Might be an option you like better."

"Bud Light's my favorite," he lied. "One of those, please."

"Suit yourself," Ann shrugged. Off she went.

As Pally returned the phone to his ear, Katie was finishing up what must have been quite a harangue, given the pitch of her voice. If he wasn't mistaken, he could hear Lily crying in the background. "...just yourself, but *all* of us! How could you think this was worth it?"

"Hang on!" he was quite shocked to find himself shouting. "Just a minute! What are you talking about? What didn't I tell you?"

"The contest!"

"...of course I told you about the contest! We were just talking about...remember the Gas-X joke?"

"How the fu..." he heard her blast the phone with a deep, ragged breath. "How can you call me and make a

191

joke when there's a man out there trying to kill you?"

"…" Pally exclaimed. He added, "…?"

THUNK, the waitress all but slammed the bottle down. Pally leapt so high his thighs hit the bottom of the table. "Take your order?" she asked him.

"Ah…" he glanced at the menu, but couldn't read a word of it. "I mean, I'll…I need another minute."

"Suit yourself," she replied. Off she went.

Pally took another minute, at the end of which Katie asked, in a much softer voice: "Did you seriously not know?"

"Oh shit!" somebody from the other end of the restaurant shouted. Pally looked up to find the shouter pointing straight at him. One of the shouter's friends acted like he recognized Pally. The others didn't…until the shouter said something to them. At that, their faces all lit up. They smiled and shook their head as they waved goodbye to the waitress and shuffled out the door.

"I didn't read the stuff I was signing," he admitted to his wife, "and I didn't watch the video when I entered. This lady in the room told me to review the stuff before I signed it, but…"

"But there was somebody outranking her who told you to sign," Katie predicted from experience.

"Mhm. But I'm starting to get the feeling I should have read the stuff, or watched the video."

"Oh, Patrick," Katie moaned. It was a sound he'd never heard her make before. Save in that one nightmare, the one from which he never woke in time.

3

Well, ok, this was kind of on him. The video, which Pally watched on his phone with the audio all the way down, so as not to further amuse the crowd falling into a lazy orbit around his booth, was pretty darn painstaking in setting out the terms of the contest.

"The lifetime supply of gas," Myrtle the animated turtle nearly sang, "is offered as a part of a fascinating and industry-disrupting new experiment in entertainment! Our lucky winner will enjoy their reward for one year, no string attached. But when that year is up," Myrtle continued as a black silhouette spun into view just beside him, "a professional contract killer will be dispatched to see if we can't shorten that lifetime. We don't want to give away *all* of our scooter juice, after all! So if you're the winner, you better hope your luck holds out!" A series of cartoonish gunshot sounds coincided with the silhouette's sliding off-screen. Pally felt his throat tightening – he didn't like that silhouette slipping off where he couldn't see it. "Make it for a year, and the hitman heads home, leaving you to enjoy your lifetime supply of gas over a much longer life!

"Now those of you who don't win, or don't enter, this is where you come in. If you see our lucky winner, film them on your phone, or on something nicer if you've got it! Then send it on over to us. If we like it, and we can use it in editing together that program we'll be making, you can win all kinds of prizes! But don't worry," Myrtle assured them as the silhouette poked its head back into frame, "these prizes won't get you in trouble." The turtle turned to the silhouette and waved its stumpy little arm. "Say, you get outta here! Don't you have a job to do?" A slide whistle and two more gunshots marked the silhouette's withdrawal.

Pally looked up to see no fewer than four phones trained on him. He didn't have it in him to even try for a brave face. "Hey!" he called to them. "I didn't know about this when I entered!"

Nobody looked up. They kept their eyes not on him, but on the him-shaped pixels on their phones.

Sweat stung his eyes. Jesus, he was dripping! Pally swiped the back of his hand across his brow, swung out of the booth and made for the door with his head ducked.

"You gotta pay!" the waitress shouted at him.

So he did. Unfortunately for Pally, she'd caught him right as he was passing the phone phalanx that defended the egress. Four, now five phones on all sides captured his hand-trembling fight to wrest a five out of his wallet. *Coverage*, was the industry term. Head so heavy it nearly threw his balance, Pally marched over to the waitress, handed her the five, and made a more successful bid for the door.

He was so distracted on the drive home that he forgot to stop off at the Tort-Oil station. A full tank at ARCO ran him about forty bucks.

4

"I mean, yeah," he explained to Katie and Lily, "I definitely feel pretty dang foolish."

His wife and daughter had been waiting for him when he got home. Apparently there had already been some calls from media outlets, as well as a visit from one proactive reporter who could only be shooed by a threat to call the police. Why Tort-Oil had released his name and identity to the public, Pally couldn't understand. If the idea was to crowd-source their *Most Dangerous Game* documentary, that was fine, he supposed, in as much as a thing like that could be fine. But nobody was going to start hunting him for another year. Why not give him the year to, uh, relax? Or try to, anyway?

"I'm thinking," Pally continued, "tomorrow I'll give them a call, explain the misunderstanding, and I'm su-"

"You can't seriously think that will work, right?" Katie asked him.

"...I guess not. Can't hurt though, can it?"

Katie shrugged.

"They would prolly use that," Lily offered.

Pally cocked an eyebrow. "Use what, sweetie?"

"I bet if you call them and ask them to stop, they'd use it on a TV episode."

"Well, honey, I'm planning on asking them very nicely for this to be what we grown-ups call *off the record*."

"But they *like* the record."

"..."

An ever-deepening nod claimed Katie's head. "You know, I think Lily's on to something there." She stilled her noggin and turned it towards Pally. "Every interaction you have with Tort-Oil, we have to assume they'll be documenting it to use in the show."

"Probably," Pally allowed, "but does that mean I shouldn't call them?"

"I think so. I wouldn't expect your call to accomplish anything, and you'd be handing them a compelling hook for their documentary."

"Um…I guess? Is that the priority though, worrying about their documentary?"

"Of course not. But it should be somewhere on the list of concerns. Why help them make their awful show in the slightest?"

"That sounds, uh…"

"Spiteful?"

"Yeah."

"Hell yes it's spiteful. Spite seems called for. Speaking of calls, I'll give Eric one, see if there's anybody outside his practice he'd trust to request a copy of the contracts you signed. Maybe there's some loophole in there that could get you out of this." She shook her head. "I can't understand how any of this is legal."

"I don't understand how I didn't hear about the murder lottery," Pally marveled. "I feel like that should have been big news."

"I heard about it," Lily told Clarence, the family's fat brown cat who could always be found in Lily's lap.

"What?" Pally tilted forward. "Where? Why didn't you tell daddy?"

"School. I didn't know you put your name in the thing." The entire bottom half of her face quivered. "I'm sorry, daddy!"

Pally knelt down and embraced his daughter, much to Clarence's audible displeasure. "It's ok, honey. It's ok. We have a big long year to work this out." He pulled back and smiled at Lily. "That's a lot of days! And your mommy happens to be very smart. It's all just a big misunderstanding. We'll have it sorted in no time." He hugged his daughter back into his chest, so that only Katie would be able to see the profound lack of conviction he had no doubt was stamped on his face.

5

He took a ribbing at work, and there was a period of about two weeks where he couldn't look out his window without having a camera pointed at him – the nicer ones with longer lenses made him feel like he was looking down the barrel of a rifle, which was, you know, not great – but within a month or two his life regained a strange kind of normalcy. There were frequent sit-downs with Eric Tillman, the Hollen's lawyer by virtue of having been a childhood friend of Katie's, as the three of them pored over the brick of pages Pally had signed *here* and *here* and also *here*, *ad infinitum*. It was all a lot of legalese that went over Pally's head, but the conclusion seemed grim: the contract was good, the killing would be kosher. By some legal jiu jitsu for which Eric couldn't hide his grudging admiration, the documents placed Pally on a Tort-Oil health insurance plan and established his eventual maybe-killer as his physician (on the contract Pally had signed, as on the copy that Eric obtained, the space for that name remained blank, which didn't seem fair given that Tort-Oil was all but skywriting Pally's social security number), thereby positioning this whole affair, with the help of quite a few other papers, as a case of physician assisted suicide. There was nothing in it detailing how Tort-Oil could possibly hire a contract killer legally, but as Eric pointed out, why would there be? That was their problem, one they had almost certainly locked up on their end.

"The good news," Eric explained in a profoundly tone-deaf way, "is that this guy has to kill you in a very specific way. He either has to force you to orally ingest secobarbital, or else intravenously get thiopental and/or propofol into your system. That's the only way the assisted suicide angle holds up."

"So he can't just shoot Pally from a distance, then?" Katie wondered eagerly.

Pally shifted in his seat. "Could we not use the third person while I'm in the room?"

"Sorry, honey. They can't just shoot, um…I need to use a third person pronoun."

"The pronoun is alright."

"Ok. They can't just shoot him from a distance?"

Pally shifted in his seat again.

"Not fatally," Eric replied, "no."

Pally frowned. "What about non-fatally?"

"In terms of what's written here," Eric replied with a Vanna White flourish over the papers, "it only specifies the means of execution. If they've found a way to get around the whole 'hiring a hitman' thing, though, I think it'd be safest to assume they've found ways to get around just about anything."

"Jesus. What if I leave the state? Go somewhere it isn't legal?"

Eric shrugged. "Same kind of deal. There's a lot of complicated paperwork here that essentially gives this guy the right to transport you across state lines. You could run, but he could knock you out, drag you back here alive, and *then* kill you."

Katie glared at the pile of papers on Eric's desk like she was trying to set them on fire with her mind. "So there's no way out of this, is what you're saying."

"I'm sorry," Eric said. "None that I can see."

Which was devastating to hear. But free fill-ups at Tort-Oil stations salved the burn, and in time the final year on Pally's lifetime lease became something like a dreadful sectional in an otherwise lovely living room. Yes, in just a few months now there would be a man coming to kill him, but Lily needed a ride to field hockey practice, the bedroom needed a good dusting, those bills weren't going to pay themselves. In a bizarre way, Pally came to take a kind of solace in his death sentence. Everybody dies and nobody knows what happens next, true, but Pally had always found much of the terror came from the unpredictability of the inevitability. One might die in forty years' time, or one might step outside to greet some improbable, *Final Destination*-esque Rube Goldberg decapitation. There was no way to know. Unless you were Pally, and there was a professional killer who'd be coming to get you on a date for which you'd had a year to prepare.

Preparation, as it happened, was something for which Pally made precious little allowance, in either time or money. Each of these he considered to be precious resources, the former prior to his death and the latter after. The fact of his death was one he could find no reason to gainsay – "I just don't see," he explained to a tearful Katie one night, "how in the heck I'm gonna not get killed by the guy who's been making a career out of it for umpteen years." Katie wanted him to fight for his life, as did Lily. It just about killed Pally to tell them no. He wouldn't waste his last year on Earth in firing ranges or self-defense dojos, and he most definitely wouldn't squander what little money he could leave his family on security cameras or rape whistles. He was a dead man, it was his own dumb fault, and that was all there was to it. "Let this serve as a lesson to you," he confided to Lily in one of his less morose moments, "*always* read the fine print."

The change came in May, a month before Mr. Silhouette was scheduled to develop human features and come a-stalking. Pally was working on the set of some middling indie drama called *Mosquito, Delaware*, the premise of which he had yet to grasp, when he overheard two coworkers, Sharon and Steve, discussing upcoming gigs. It was a common sort of conversation to hear amongst the below-the-line grunts on a professional LA set, just the type of exchange Pally would ordinarily tune out. For some reason, though, he was tuned in when he heard Steve say he would be running sound on "that show about Pally".

Pally remembered standing a few yards away and hearing this, and he remembered being right in Steve's personal space and demanding to know "WHAT" in a rather holistic and all-encompassing way, but he didn't remember the intervening moments.

"*Fuck*," Steve mumbled. They'd always been on good terms, Pally and Steve, and the former hoped that explained the latter's sudden shoulder-slouching shame at having been caught out.

"Why the heck, er, *hell* did you take that gig?!" Pally demanded with uncommon (and, to himself, incomprehensible) fury. "I thought we were friends!"

Steve, a camera operator not used to being on the receiving end of such scrutiny, grimaced at far wall of the soundstage, to which Sharon was hastily decamping. "A gig's a gig," he mumbled without conviction.

"Didn't you turn down a gig working on *Crossroads*?"

"Well, yeah," Steve shrugged, "but that was for… well, I wasn't as strapped for cash then."

"Didn't you just work on the new goddamned *Batman* movie?"

"It was just called *The Goddamned Batman*, but, yeah."

"Didn't pay you enough, then?"

201

"Jesus Christ," Steve exploded, "yeah, it paid fine! But I took the gig on your show ages ago, before it was *your* show! They hadn't even announced it to the public yet! They've been hashing this shit out with the union for years now, I just put my name in and forgot about it!"

A little bell tinkled in the furthest reaches of Pally's mind. Something about that wasn't right. "Local 600?"

"Yeah. They wanted to do the thing non-union, like any other reality show, but th-"

Pally released his grip on Steve's lapels, which was how he realized he had been gripping Steve's lapels. "Why are they talking to a cinematographer's union? I thought the whole point was everyday schmoes were filming me and sending it in?"

Steve shrugged. "I don't know, man. Something the honchos worked out. But they're gonna have some pro shooters…um, I mean camera ops on the gig as well. Make sure they get at least *some* usable footage. They've gotta protect their investment, you know how it is."

"I guess so," Pally said, though not necessarily to Steve. That tinkling bell in the back of his mind was straight-up pissing on the walls now. This revelation, as well as the urgency with which Steve begged Pally not to tell anybody he'd told him, he was NDA'd six ways from Sunday, it would be the end of his career if anybody heard he'd spilled the beans, etc., all meant… something. Pally couldn't put his finger on it, but fortunately, when he brought the tale home that night, Katie could.

"That's awfully convenient," Katie mumbled, a slight smile alighting upon her face.

Pally leaned forward, eager to hear what she'd spotted. "What is?"

"Well, I was thinking about this after our last conversation with Eric. The phrasing of the contract that allows Tort-Oil to hire a guy to kill you hinges on assisted suicide being legal in California. At first, given how they've covered all their bases and then some with those documents, I assumed it was just a coincidence that the winner hailed from one of those states. I figured, if somebody from, I don't know, South Dakota or wherever won, they would have them move to the nearest state that allowed assisted suicide. But...doesn't it seem awfully coincidental that not only is their winner from one of the six states in which they can pull off this stunt, but he's from the one state that's got all the contentious unions that, if whatever legalistic mumbo jumbo is making this happen forces Tort-Oil to work with them, almost *certainly* want to keep as many jobs local as they can?"

Pally stared at his third glass of Pinot Grigio (nearly ready for a fourth) and the funhouse-mirror image of his wife that floated within. Sufficiently disoriented, he returned his gaze to the genuine article. "I don't know if I follow you."

Katie planted her elbows on the table and chopped at it with her palms. "The contest was run nationally. I checked. Open to anybody from every state, even the territories. What are the odds, out of such a massive entrant pool, they happened to pick a winner who ticked two very big boxes for them?"

"California's a big state," Pally advocated infernally.

"I would bet you anything, they're doing something with all those emails they racked up. Selling the data to spammers or else using them to send their own spam, the kind of sh…" she glanced at Lily. "*Stuff* companies do all the time now. Lily, don't put Clarence on the table."

"Are you saying what I think you're saying?"

"That depends," Katie grinned. "What do you think I'm saying?"

"…I don't know. I was hoping you'd just keep talking."

Katie sighed, then sat back as though she'd just said *checkmate*. "I'm saying I think Tort-Oil ran a scam here. They teased the entire country with a prize they only ever intended to award to someone from California, so they could get as much information as possible to use in whatever way they wanted." She picked up her fork and prodded her otherwise untouched meal. "I'm going to give Eric a call tomorrow, run this by him. But if there's anything in the contract at all that demands a contest run in good faith, and we can somehow demonstrate – or at least imply with something more concrete than me shooting…sorry, um, well you know, than me just talking sh…*stuff* around the dinner table – that this contract *wasn't* executed…sorry honey, uh, *activated?*…in good faith, maybe we can beat it. We could get you out of this."

"YAY!" Lily screamed, sending both her parents (and Clarence) halfway to the ceiling.

"Wow!" Pally exclaimed once he'd regained his composure. "Great thinking! You're a genius!" He lunged at his wife and kissed her so thoroughly and extensively that Lily eventually got tired of saying 'ew'. "My only question," he finally gasped, "is, would I get to keep the lifetime supply of gas?"

"Honey," Katie laughed, "I'll pay for the gas."

6

Pally knew the anniversary of his most unfortunate lucky break was coming up when the cameras started coming out again. In line for lunch, walking his groceries to the car, taking Clarence to the vet, there always seemed to be a phone or two floating in his peripheral vision. *Don't waste your time*, he wanted to tell them, *if you aren't up on your union dues.*

Fortunately, it wasn't all bad news. Katie had apparently had a highly encouraging phone call with Eric, exuding a newfound optimism which Pally got to share once they made it to Tillman's office.

"For the most part," he told them for Pally's benefit, "this thing is impeccably phrased. They leave themselves all kinds of wiggle room. There's this one clause, though," he flipped through page after page until he found the one he wanted, "that explicitly refers to a 'wholly randomized' selection process. Now, it's a clause that deals with some of the more arcane nuances of their foreign syndication deal, but I think, *think*, that we might be able to domino this into the whole contract getting thrown out.

"What we need," he continued far more coldly, as if to intercept the enthusiasm he knew had been forthcoming, "is something better than conjecture. I know you're aware of this," he nodded to Katie, "we discussed it on the phone." He hefted the contract in his hand and waved it towards Pally. "But I need something concrete I can stick to this thing, if we want to get any kind of arbitration going. Is there somebody you could talk to, someone who might be able to confirm, *on the record* – that means no anonymous sources, Pally – that the process by which they selected a winner was less than quote, 'wholly randomized', unquote?"

Pally's first instinct was to say 'no', which was a reversal from the enthusiastic 'yes' by which he had lived his life until it won him a contract with a professional hitman. But, upon further consideration… he realized that this was yet another thing to which he could, in fact, say yes.

7

Julia Berman, head of PR, had left Tort-Oil in October. Pally liked to imagine that it was a principled stand she was taking on his behalf, in response to the injustice of allowing a man to sign his life away, knowing full well that he didn't even know *half* well. He liked to imagine all that, but in truth he could accept that his situation was likely one of many straws that had been piled atop the camel's back.

Perhaps if it was a large enough straw, though…the camel might be compelled to help? However that metaphor wrapped up, Pally's only hope of getting some inside dirt that might render the contract null and void was the decidedly un-ungulate woman who had shown him some measure of compassion in the boardroom nearly one year ago.

As it wasn't going to be a simple matter of calling Tort-Oil and getting passed up the corporate ladder, assuming that would have been a simple matter to begin with, Pally would need to exercise some ingenuity in tracking Ms. Berman down. Unfortunately, if there were two things notably lacking from Pally's life, they were exercise and ingenuity. So when his first and last stop of googling "Julia Berman phone number" yielded no useful results, he leaned back into his ergonomic computer chair, folded his arms and declared "that was my best idea."

Of course, it *wasn't* his best idea – his best idea was marrying Katie, who had a far less passive relationship to fate than Pally. Identifying a bargaining chip that never would have occurred to her husband, Katie called up the *Los Angeles Times* and offered them an exclusive interview with either herself, should her husband be killed, or both she and Pally should he survive, to be granted the day after the contract on her husband's life lapsed. This scoop was contingent on somebody getting her a current number or address by which Tort-Oil's ex-head of PR Julia Berman could be contacted. Mere hours after Katie placed that call, some investigative whiz-kid rang back with Julia's cell number.

"What would I do without you?!" Pally shouted as he bear-hugged Katie and spun them both around in circles.

"Good thing we don't have to find out," she replied in a less-than-full-bodied laugh.

Seeing as she was on such a roll, Pally had hoped Katie would make the call to Julia – he was awkward on phone calls even when he *wasn't* asking someone for information that, should she grant it, would probably constitute some kind of corporate espionage. But Katie insisted his be the voice Julia heard when she picked up, and with a bit of prodding from Lily (likely a result of prodding from Katie), Pally was made to see reason. He punched in the digits, hit the green button, brought the phone to his ear, and listened to the ring. A second ring. A th-

"Hello?"

Pally recognized the voice immediately. It hit that same note of concern now as it did a year ago, as though she knew precisely who was calling her...or had been waiting and hoping for his call all this time.

"Ahem," Pally began. "Julie Berman?"

"Julia. Patrick Hollen."

"Jul...no...wait a second, *I'm* Patrick Hollen!"

"And I'm Julia Berman." He could hear her smiling over the phone. "I recognized your voice."

"Oh. Right. Um." He looked to Katie, who was

making a hanging up gesture with her hand. Ah, right. "Any chance we might be able to talk not on the phone?"

Julia sighed. "Do you suspect your phone might be tapped, Mr. Hollen?"

"Pally."

A brief pause. "I'm surprised you still consider me a friend."

"Friend enough, if you've a mind to help me. Whaddyasay?"

"I don't live in California anymore. I moved to Kentucky."

"...why?"

"Because I don't know anybody who lives in Kentucky. If there's something I can do to help you, name it and I'll try. I feel awful for not being clearer than I was in that room. About what you were...doing. I'm not sure just how much help I *can* be, seeing as I've no real access to anyone or anything at Tort-Oil anymore...but I'll do what I can."

This was one of those moments when Pally would likely have had something to say, were this discussion happening in person. But as he was hearing this heartfelt confession while staring at a framed picture of a bird on his wall, his attention torn between feeling touched by Julia's solidarity and wondering where the hell that framed picture of a bird had come from and why they had decided to hang it on their wall in the first place, Pally's response to Julia's candor was "Cool, sounds good. Erm. I mean, thank you!"

Fortunately, Julia sounded more amused than put out by Pally's response. "So, *Pally*...how can I help you?"

8

"I can't help you," Julia replied after hearing Pally's pitch for a way out. "I'm truly sorry, but to be the head of PR is to be insulated, indeed *isolated*, from the kinds of corner-cutting that no doubt define each and every decision a corporation as large as Tort-Oil makes. If I don't know how the sausage gets made, I can assure everyone that it's only the highest-grade meats without technically *lying* to them, if you see what I mean. I can speculate and assume right along with you, but nothing I say or know could constitute a breach of 'good faith' or anything of the sort."

"Hello Ms. Berman," Katie said to the phone, which was now on speaker and sitting on the kitchen table, "this is Katie, Pally's wife. Isn't there anybody you could call who might be able to give us *any* information? Just a shred of evidence that the winner wasn't chosen entirely at random?"

Julia made all the noises of someone pretending to think about something to which they already know the answer: sighing, tongue-clicking, lip-flapping. Katie and Pally exchanged less-than-optimistic glances.

"Not without raising hackles," Julia finally replied. "I have a few friends who still work at Tort-Oil, but they're mostly in the PR department – they kept us pretty well compartmentalized – so I doubt they would have access to information I wouldn't have. Besides, there's a company-wide memorandum that lists me as *persona non grata* until the conclusion of this little 'contest'. Based on our last interaction, I think they fully anticipated you would reach out to me at some point, or I to you."

Katie placed her arm on Pally's back and rubbed. Her husband stared at the phone as though it were Clarence in the middle of a Shakespearean, chest-clutching death scene. So slack was his body that each of Katie's rubs sent him jostling in whatever direction her hand was heading.

"So what do I do?" he asked the phone.

Sighing, tongue-clicking, lip-flapping. The noises stopped, and Julia said "you try to stay alive."

9

To be given hope and have it dashed was worse than never having had hope at all. Where he had once achieved an almost zen-like resignation to his fate, Pally now sank into a deep, depressive morass. The courage to face death had abandoned him; now, he wanted nothing more than to lie with his face buried in a pillow and wait for oblivion to come bonk him on the back of the head.

Understandably enough, this was distressing to Katie and Lily. It was only their repeated entreaties that got him out of bed, over to the computer and onto the internet in search of sanctuary. Much as it pained him, the fact was that he needed to leave home. *He* was the lucky winner of the contest, and so *he* was the one in trouble. The only way he could endanger his wife and daughter would be to have them by his side. Nor could he countenance putting them out of the house, consoling himself with their safety as some gun-toting lunatic shot up the only home Lily had ever known. No, it was on him to leave. So the question naturally followed: where to?

The idea of hopping in the car and using his free Tort-Oil gas to stay on the move had a certain 90's thriller appeal, but Pally knew himself well enough to recognize the cat and mouse game was his to lose. He would get sleepy, or hungry, or his nervous bowels would get the best of him, and as soon as he stopped, it'd be lights out. Besides, he'd spent the better part of a decade wrestling with hemorrhoids, which he had only recently brought under any kind of control. Days on end sitting in the car, probably sweating bullets all the while? No way.

Besides, he thought to himself as he recalled Katie's suggestion to not call the company directly, using Tort-Oil to make his escape was probably just what they wanted. A perverse kind of viral advertising, brand synergy, all that nonsense. He could just see the fifteen-second spots now, fast-cuts of his sweat-drenched mug hunched over the wheel, shifting uncomfortably in his seat, with some overpaid celebrity (whose voice most people wouldn't even recognize) saying things like "when the stakes are mortal...", pan in to the Tort-Oil station, "...go see Myrtle!" Then they would animate the big Myrtle logo they have spinning atop every Tort-Oil station so that it would wink, and the wink would make a little *ding* sound, and then a rocket-propelled grenade would slam into the side of Pally's car and the world would explode.

Only no it wouldn't. He had to get killed by chemicals. The rest of the ad would stand, though, and Julia's pals in the PR department would look at it and wonder if there was a way to work in more four-quadrant appeal.

Running without a goal was suicide, and he had no intention of going to visit friends, thereby endangering *them*. Granted, given the extremely narrow parameters by which he could be legally killed by this hitman, it was probably unlikely that he would be spraying roadside motels with Rambo-sized guns. More than *probably* unlikely, actually. But accidents had a way of happening around Patrick Hollen, and he wasn't willing to risk anybody else being placed in danger for this stupid little murder contest-cum-TV show.

That didn't leave him with a lot of options, though.

Pally and Katie had turned the family dinners into brainstorming sessions, much to the chagrin of Lily, who wanted to talk about all the exciting new things she was learning in school, like maps and cursive. She held her peace at first, as each attempt to change the topic of conversation was met with a curt "not now, honey", but as the days of fruitless spitballing crawled by, Lily grew too frustrated to keep her tongue in check.

"Call the news people again," she rumbled in the middle of yet another 'no that won't work but maybe *this*' monologue from her mother.

"Huh?" Katie and Pally wondered in synchrony.

Lily flipped her hair like she couldn't *believe* the simpletons in her presence. "Mom called the news people one time and they helped. So call more news people for more help."

"That's not really how that works," Pally informed her gently.

Katie, however, saw what her daughter was saying at once. "That's an amazing idea!"

"It was your idea first," Lily offered humbly, not because she was feeling humble but because she had been raised well.

Pally studied his placemat as though it would be transforming into a treasure map any second now. He looked to his wife, not needing to say "I don't get it" because by this point that was implied.

"This is news," she explained, "this contest, you, people are interested in it. If there's a way we can…" she trailed off and studied her placemat as though it already *was* a treasure map. A grin crawled across her face; she'd found the X that marked the spot. "It's always down to the contract," she mumbled as she launched herself up from the table and hustled out of the kitchen.

Pally turned to his daughter. "Can you explain to me what's going on?"

"It's always down to the contract," Lily explained matter-of-factly.

10

"Imagine if I were billing you for all of this," Eric chuckled ruefully as the Hollens rung him on speaker the following day. "Ok, here's what I found. There's no distributor specified; they're producing this on 'spec', as it were, though I don't imagine they'll have a hard time landing a network. What *is* specified, and it's a little convoluted but I've put my most pedantic underlings on it and I believe they've hammered this out accurately, is that Tort-Oil are promising exclusive rights to the project, domestically, for one year following the broadcast of the first episode, or of the first part of the movie, or however they choose to edit it. At that point the exclusivity lifts, presumably so they can add ten minutes of footage, shop it around to someone else and cash in again on a 'director's cut' or whatever. No such guarantees are tendered to foreign markets. Does that answer your question?"

Katie leaned over the phone. "That sounds like it's about the product itself though. I'm asking about the subject. If Pally were to get involved in another documentary covering the same period of time as Tort-Oil's, by which I mean right *now*, would he or...*we*, if he... would this household be in danger of being sued?"

"Short answer is yes, if you were to be involved with the rival documentary in any official capacity. Now, an *unauthorized* documentary in which you could be plausibly said to have had no direct involvement...that lives in a grey area called Not Your Problem. Whoever's name was attached to that product, they might get a few unfriendly letters, but it wouldn't come back to you."

The smile on Katie's face told Pally they were in some kind of business. As he was still somewhat unclear on what his wife had in mind, he could only smile along and try to fix his heart to match.

"Thank you," Katie told the phone. They exchanged the back-end pleasantries, have a good one talk soon okay bye bye, and ended the call.

"Are we in business?" Pally asked.

Katie nodded big and kissed him on the cheek. "We are!"

"That's great! So, uh, can you tell me what kind of business we're in?"

She threw her arms up, smiled big as her nod and shouted "show business!"

11

The idea was appealing idiotic, nearly matching the absurdity of Pally's present predicament. Katie wanted to find another documentary crew to produce a documentary about Pally's escape from Tort-Oil, their contract killer and the attendant documentary, the idea being that this would give Pally access to a vast network of resources and support. The catch, of course, was that Pally couldn't be *officially* involved with the production of said documentary, so any assistance tendered to him would have to be done indirectly, or at least through an improbable number of intermediaries. But how would that work? How could anybody help ferry Pally to safety without becoming clearly, self-evidently involved with him?

This problem proved intractable, uncrackable by even the most specific of online searches ('rich people helpful private jet generous charity' was Pally's best attempt, which yielded a great many results but no actual answers), until Pally had the kind of epiphany one only has whilst twisting one's bedsheets into topography from the fetal position.

He swung himself out of bed so quickly he got a headrush, and so had to support himself with hands on the walls as he staggered towards the desk from which his laptop had taken to mocking him. His ass had hardly hit the seat before his fingers were pounding away at the keys. Within ten minutes, he'd found exactly what he was looking for.

"Wow," Katie marveled when Pally showed her the next morning. "This is a great idea."

"You sound surprised," Pally deadpanned. He reached down to stroke Clarence, who was rubbing up against his ankle.

Apparently inspired by her husband's feline ministrations, Katie rubbed Pally's back, but didn't actually respond to what he'd said. Instead, she asked "have you reached out to them?"

"I don't think they're the sorts to have phone and

email they check on the regular. Looks like you just kinda show up."

"I thought you said they did videos, though."

"They do. They love their videos."

Katie reached out and slid her fingers across the trackpad. For a tech-averse survivalist compound in the middle of Nowhere, Arizona (which, as far as Katie was concerned, was just *Arizona*), they sure had a glossy website. Graphic-heavy, as was all the rage with the plug-and-play web design services, but it looked good, as long as climate-contradicting camo fatigues and comically oversized assault weapons were your thing.

She dragged the cursor to one of the video thumbnails and clicked. A man with the shape and charisma of a whiskey barrel appeared on screen, clutching a sheathed hunting knife to his chest and staring directly into the camera.

"The Desert Island compound ain't about kooky conspiracies or lizard people. We ain't crazy down here, 'less you think keepin' an eye on a dwindlin' water supply is crazy. Or 'less you think frettin' over this great nation's vulnerable power grids is crazy. Or 'less you think not wantin' government to watch us through our laptops while we yank it is crazy. That last one you can just use a little strip of tape or somethin', but for the rest, ain't no amount of tape's gonna protect you. The tape goes on the little camera, I oughta specify. It ain't, uh…anyway. That's how come I'm here at Desert Island." He paused and took a breath. "Hi, my name's Brimley Furlough, and here are my top five albums I brought with me to Desert Island. Number one is *Chicago II* by Chicago. I actually brought this one on accident, but it ain't bad. Number two i-"

"They look a little..." Kate interrupted the video.

Pally watched her scrutinizing Mr. Furlough on the video. "Soft?"

She nodded. "Are they gonna be able to protect you?"

"Hang on." Pally took his hand off Clarence (much to the cat's audible disapproval) and clicked through to a different video, this one of Brimley and his Desert Island buddies on the firing range, moving and shooting like men half their age.

"Holy shit. I almost feel bad for the contract killer guy."

"Ha, ha."

Thump. Pally and Katie both started. *Thump* again. Just Clarence jumping against the wall, exercising one of his occasional cat fascinations with things only he could see.

"When do you want to leave?" Katie asked.

Thump.

"Well, that depends on-"

Thump.

Pally looked back to Clarence, leaping against the wall. Only this time he let his eyes track a little higher.

Thump.

To the red laser pointer dot scanning across the wall.

Thump.

Without taking his eyes off the dot, he asked Katie:

219

"What day is it?"

ThunKRAAAAAASHHH replied the window behind Pally. It exploded inward, the majority of the glass fortunately falling straight down rather than launching into the room. As Katie all but wrapped her frozen husband in a headlock and dragged him to the ground, Pally looked at the wall where the dot had been.

There was a hole there now.

"I thought he wasn't allowed to use guns!" Pally screamed.

"Non-fatally!" Katie replied.

"Where's Lily?"

"Bed!"

"Thank fuck! I mean, Jiminy Crickets! I should have set a calendar alert on my phone or something, huh?"

"I assumed we'd just sort of remember the date."

"Me too."

Another gunshot punched through the wall just beneath the window, where the hitman must have assumed Pally fell. And, if he had been watching, he would have had to assume that was also where Katie had fallen as well.

So much for not caring about collateral damage.

"MOOOOOM!" Lily cried from her room.

There was only responsible, logical, fatherly thing to do in this situation. Instead, Pally made a high-pitched whining sound, because that was a lot easier.

"What's wrong?" Katie scrambled on top of him. "Are you hit?"

"I have to go! If he's gonna shoot up the house, the

only thing I can do to keep you two safe is to just go!"

"Take the car!" she replied, which wasn't exactly what he'd been hoping to hear. He'd have liked something along the lines of *oh no*, or *isn't there some other way*, or *please don't go, how will I survive*, which admittedly didn't make a lot of sense but at least *one* perfunctory bit of resistance to his heroism would have been appreciated. Then he could have resisted *that*, which would have made him extra heroic. Ah, well.

"Ok!" he replied.

"And be careful!" She grabbed the collar of his shirt, pulled him in and kissed him hard. "I love you!"

"I love you too!" Pally cried. He slapped his hand to the outside of his pocket – he could feel the car keys in there. No excuse for delay then; he had to make a break for it.

Keeping low, he crept out into the hall and halfway towards Lily's room.

"Lily, honey!" he called.

"Yeah?" she responded.

"Lily, it's not safe for me to come into your room. Stay in bed. I just need you to know that I love you, and everything I've done, I did for you."

"Dad?"

"Yes dear?"

"Could you ask Mom to come in?"

"…ok. I love you, Lily."

"Ok. I love you too."

Pally crept back towards his room. "Lily wants you to go see her."

"Right now?"

"I mean, probably once the gun guy is gone."

"Will do. Good luck."

"Yep. Thanks. Love you."

"Love you too."

It was on that note of oppressive banality that Pally bade his family farewell. He'd certainly never imagined parting from his loved ones on precisely these terms, but as anyone with hostages to fortune is wont to do on long, dark nights, he had played out comparable scenarios in his nightmares. They were always marked by a great many tearful embraces, a gnashing of the teeth and rending of the garments, real slow-motion, opera-scored type stuff. Grief as performance. Really moving.

That he was denied this only intensified Pally's determination to survive the year. There was no *way* that was going to be the last time he ever saw his family again. The farewell hadn't been nearly dramatic enough.

12

He swung around the tussock at the base of his banister and encountered an empty foyer. The coward was sniping from across the street, then. Maybe because he wouldn't be allowed to break and enter? The knife's edge of legality upon which this whole venture teetered was narrower than Pally could make sense of.

So he opted to turn to topics of which sense *could* be made, by a mind such as his. Let's see…given which way the bullets had torn through the window and wall of his office, the gunman must have been on the Eastern side of the house. Which was where the garage was, natch.

CRACK, another gunshot. He heard Katie and Lily scream from upstairs, and chastised himself for thinking *now* that *was dramatic!*

His second thought, of course, was that the asshole still thought Pally was upstairs, and so was still snapping off shots through the office window.

Or was this a bluff, meant to pressure Pally into revealing himself?

Pally congratulated himself for such a strategic thought, but his elation was short lived, because it all came out to the same thing: a gun was being fired at his house, and his family was screaming for their lives.

"No, Pally," he sighed in falsetto, "don't go!"

"I have to," he assured himself in a rotund *basso*, "it's the only way to keep you safe."

"I love you, Daddy!" he bleated in a screech that, were it not his own daughter he was impersonating, would have been perceived as a pretty savage burn.

"I love you too," the deep-chested Pally replied. "Farewell, my loves."

With that, he pushed off his heel and ran for the garage door at a loping crouch that, had he been covered in ping-pong balls, would have gotten him a featured extra role in a *Planet of the Apes* movie.

He swung the door open, took the two steps down at a leap, thought about doing a forward roll to the car, remembered he couldn't do a forward roll, landed hard on his knees, and see-sawed onto his face. "Blurgh," he spat as he pushed himself to his feet. A quick survey of his face turned up a tender spot but no broken skin or bones, so he labeled his acrobatics an overall success and climbed in to his car, stuffed the keys in the ignition and cranked.

To his credit, a rather larger tactical error occurred to him as he committed it, rather than strictly after the fact.

Pally drove a 2005 Honda CR-V. It was a warhorse of a car, one that defied time and the elements by continuing to run. One of the ways it showed its age, though, was in the phlegmatic hacking and wheezing by which it lurched to life before each drive. This was not a car with an indoor voice. Consequently, it could likely be heard outdside of the garage. Which would be a headstart for anybody keeping an ear out.

Immediately after clicking the garage door remote, Pally realized the mistake.

He looked in the rearview mirror. The garage door staggered up up up, revealing a pair of rather serious looking combat boots.

Once again, Pally couldn't help but view this moment in his life as though through a lens. *This is well cinematic*, he thought just before the shooting started.

A vicious, viscous roar flooded the garage. Bullets speckled the door from the outside, riding the newly admitted beams of sunlight straight through the back of Pally's car. His rear windshield said *thk thk*, and then belched itself out of existence. Seat stuffing flew into the air and somehow remained there, now falling in slow motion like flakes in a snowglobe that somebody was still shaking the hell out of.

For what felt like an eternity, Pally could do nothing but hunch his shoulders, half-shield his head with his hands, shake and scream. Then something clipped his neck. Warm soaked into his shirt. His mouth was full of pennies.

He looked at the rearview mirror again. The garage door was only up to the gunman's knees. And he was still shooting.

Pally punched the car into reverse and slammed on the gas. He was going to back out of his own garage door, and probably run over a gun guy who was trying to shoot him dead. True, this was an experience he could have done without. But now that it was happening, what was the harm in simply acknowledging that it was kind of awesome?

Ah right, well, there was the neck wound. Didn't seem to be bleeding too badly though. Probably just glass.

The spare tire on the back of the CR-V hit the garage door and caught. The garage door tutted loudly once, twice, and then quit.

Shit.

Pally threw the car in drive and put the pedal to the plastic well cover.

The warhorse scooted forward.

He slammed the brake before the car had a chance to plow into the concrete wall in front of him.

IDENTICAL PIGS

The shooting outside stopped. Maybe the gun guy was getting into a different position, so that when Pally came out, he would be zooming right into a line of fire?

Obviously that's what was happening. Which begged the question: keep doing what he was doing, which probably wouldn't get much further than "fuck up the garage door a whole bunch from the inside", or change his approach?

Solid follow-up question: what other approaches did he have? Running sure as hell wasn't on the menu, seeing as fried chicken and creamy pastas so often had been. It was drive or die. Probably both. But surely he could make it further than his garage, right? That wouldn't be...

...

That wouldn't be dramatic.

What had Steve said? Tort-Oil hired a professional production crew to protect their investment. And Eric had said they were currently deciding between releasing this whole thing as a series, or a movie. And Katie had quite rightly pointed out that every move he made needed to be considered from the perspective of how it would play on camera...

Clarence had had time to jump at the laser dot on the wall, what, five or six times before he and Katie had noticed it? And the shooting hadn't started until they acknowledged it...

This was performance. Maybe not the whole thing, but certainly this opening salvo. He had discovered first hand that, left to its own devices, reality was often hopelessly anticlimactic. Which was fair enough, seeing as climaxes came at the ends of things, whereas reality just sort of chugged along without any consideration of narrative or theme. The world could often muster up no grander a finale than *take the car*. Tort-Oil would surely settle for nothing so banal.

Equally banal: the subject of their documentary being gunned down on the very first day, the very first *hour*, after a year's worth of hype. And that wasn't even taking in to account that seven maybe eight maybe *nine* figures of legal fees incurred in the drafting of their gargantuan stay-out-of-jail fine-print anthology. No way, no how was this guy shooting to kill so early in the day.

Pally kicked at the car door, which did little except hurt his leg and hip. Hopefully nobody had been filming *that*, he mused as he popped the handle with his hand, which wasn't nearly urgent or exciting enough but it would have to do, and tumbled out of the car, sprinted out of the garage, and barreled into the bathroom to inspect his neck in the mirror.

He might as well have cut himself shaving. In fact, the mere act of seeing how small his wound was diminished the pain considerably.

Ok. So. Yes. He was quite confident that, should he walk right out the front door, the gunman would not actually shoot at him – at least, not with the intention of hitting him. The question was whether or not *quite* was confident enough to get him out the front door. Wasn't it just as likely they'd *love* to have him dead on day one? What a funny headline *that* would make. *EPIC FAIL,* as the kids had stopped saying a while ago.

No, that wasn't the question. The question was: what other choice did he have?

Pally took a deep breath as he rose to his feet, squaring his shoulders the best he could. He tiptoed to the front door, like the gunman was asleep upstairs and Pally was trying not to wake him up, and peered out the little windows set on either side of the doorframe.

The street was jam-packed with cell phones attached to people-shaped tripods. None of them were moving, or jostling for a better angle. They were all just standing there, filming...*him*. Not Pally *him*. The other *him*.

The gun guy.

Pally watched...*him* pace back and forth on the street, as though there weren't a wall of little lenses right behind him. The gun guy was...too much. He had sunglasses, black hair slicked straight back, a slate-grey three piece suit bulging atop the bulk of a Kevlar vest (like Pally was gonna start shooting back), and a jaw so chiseled, the guy could probably just use that to slice Pally in half. In his hand was some kind of big, angry gun. Despite the number of movie sets Pally had worked on, and so the number of prop guns he had been exposed to, he knew jack shit about them. Some were small and went *pop pop pop*, some were big and went *babababa*. This was a *babababa* one.

He blinked and finally caught the association that had been dancing along the periphery of his mind. *Heat.* This guy looked like he was doing some half-assed *Heat* bank robbery cosplay; the only thing he was missing was an attention to detail. In fact, the more closely Pally scrutinized him, the more certain he became that the look on the guy's face was discomfort. This was not his typical getup.

It was a *costume*.

That cinched it. This guy was decked out so far beyond what a contract killer with an eye towards contract killing would actually wear, because Tort-Oil was more concerned with it looking good than actually working. For now, at least. But now was all Pally could worry about. And right now, it was showtime.

So he opened his front door and walked right on out.

13

Everything over the past year, the stress on himself and his family, the time he'd wasted trying to find ways out of this predicament, the dubious place in reality TV history he was doomed to occupy whether he survived or not; all of this was very nearly rendered *worth it* by the look of supreme gormlessness blasted across every single face out there, including and *especially* Gun Guy's.

Pally summoned up a confidence he neither possessed nor deserved, strode to the end of his walkway, stood arms akimbo and glared.

Gun Guy had stuffed his finger in his ear and was mumbling something. Talking with producers, no doubt. Behind him, the folks with the phones rumbled to life: crouching, rising on tippy-toes, turning their phones this way and that (including on themselves; Pally imagined Gun Guy getting confused and doing the same with his gun, an improbable but nonetheless amusing daydream).

The first stage of his Dramatic Character Reveal was a success. Too bad for him that he was only now thinking of it as the "first stage" – what came next? Should he say something defiant? Stride confidently up to Gun Guy and, what, give him the finger? Showmanship was far from Pally's forte.

He brought his attention back to Gun Guy just in time to see him nodding, removing his finger from his ear, and lifting his gun towards Pally.

So maybe the producers were going for the *funny headline* angle. Shit.

Strategy was the first thing to be jettisoned; Pally broke hard to the right and bolted just as the *babababa* cracked in his left ear. The windows on the ground floor of his home exploded to his right, giving him a few more cut-myself-shaving nicks for the road.

Pally cut (nicked?) around the side of his house, stumbling through the dry grass and nearly taking the low hill he called a backyard like a runaway hula-hoop. He caught himself and kept his legs pumping straight into the yard behind his, which belonged to folks called...oh, who the fuck knew? This was LA; the only people who knew their neighbors were celebrities and prisoners. He glanced in the window as he passed the house to see helicopter footage of himself braking hard to the right and bolting just as the machine gun fire started. Terrific. The helicopter's presence only now became apparent to him, rotors overhead being naught but white noise. He raised his hand to flick the bird at the bird, but his foot caught on the tiny rock wall surrounding a garden full of dead plants and he was back to stumbling.

Just as he regained his balance (unaccustomed to running, he had never fully appreciated how precious yet febrile his equilibrium was), the dirt at his feet giggled, shooting up in waist-high spurts. The *babababa* behind him followed a split-second later.

A humming whine escaped his throat as he banked left and kept running at an ever-diminishing pace. Air felt like fire in his lungs, shredding his throat. His heart was thrumming in his temples, behind his eyes. He had to get off of his feet as soon as possible, or his heart was going to explode. But how? He didn't know any-body in this damn neighborhood, and he couldn't exactly hotwire a car. So where was he going to find, as people dressed like Gun Guy in the movies tended to say, *wheels*?

It took only three more running steps for the answer to come loose and start rattling around Pally's skull, right along with his brain. Without his speed flagging (well, more than it already was), he wrestled his phone out of his pocket, thumbed the fingerprint reader to unlock it, thumbed it again, mumbled "heck", pressed it to get the keycode option up, pressed it again, swiped over to the lock screen dashboard, pressed the icon for *Zyp*, pressed "use keycode option", entered his keycode, stumbled on the dip of the curb, fell hard into the street, watched his phone skitter to the other side and smack into the far curb, pushed himself to his feet, ran for his phone, picked it up, ensured it wasn't broken by force of habit, then resumed running and called himself a Zyp car.

14

His driver's name was *Farrow*, her favorite drivin' tunes were *Whatever fits the vibe* and she was from *LA born and raised!*. She looked either Hispanic or Native American, Pally couldn't really tell, but either way he was totally fine with it, it wasn't even a thing, he was just noting. Whatever she was, not that she was a *what*, but just…anyway, she drove a Kia Soul and had a 4.8 rating, which was not necessarily great, but definitely acceptable. Even now, Pally would likely have cancelled on a driver with anything less than a 4.4, because holy *shit* what did they do to get a 4.4?

The advantage that Zyp had over other ridesharing apps was quite simple: in addition to being able to set a pickup marker, as with the competition, Zyp offered the option of tracking the phone as a pickup marker. As long as you weren't moving faster than the average walking pace – which, given how long Pally had been running, he probably wasn't anymore – you could begin walking towards your destination, or towards a more easily accessible street, and the Zyp car would come find you.

So Pally kept hoofing his way down the street, bracing for the crack of an automatic announcing a thousand lead friends come to tickle him to bits, until a massive blue blob swallowed his peripheral vision. The blob honked. Pally shrieked.

As he turned, the blob became a Kia Soul. The driver's window buzzed down to reveal a vaguely familiar, ethnically ambiguous face. "You Patrick?" Farrow asked in a rather neutral newscaster accent that didn't have much by way of identifying markers.

"Yes!" he gasped. He dove for the door of the still-moving car and only realized just how sweaty he'd gotten as he slid onto the dry, hopefully scotchgarded upholstery. "Sorry about the wet," was all he managed to say.

"Where are you going?" she turned around and smiled at him as though he was the third glaze-faced man who'd lain prostrate in her car this afternoon (were this the evening, he might have genuinely considered that he was).

"Huh?"

"You haven't input a destination." She seemed to trace his entire form with her eyes, which promptly lit up. "Aren't you the guy?"

"Yes," he wheezed, "I'm the guy. Please just drive and I'll input a destination."

"I'm not gonna get shot, am I?" she asked this like somebody who knew there was a fake snake in the jar of peanuts they were about to open, but wanted to play along anyway.

"Not if you drive," he advised her.

Taking the funereal tone in his voice, she turned around and drove.

Pally shimmied himself upright in his seat and buckled the belt. *Click it or ticket*, his brain decided to think just then. Stupid brain.

"Thank you," he managed once he'd gotten at least *some* of his breath back.

Farrow shrugged. "For driving? It's the gig."

"You could have put me out on the street and zoomed off."

Her eyes met his in the rearview. "Nah, this'll be fun. I'm hoping I get some royalties from the show, you know?"

"Me too," Pally mumbled as he watched the neighborhood tick by.

15

Farrow asked for quiet as she merged onto the 101, but then resumed the conversation just where she'd left it off: "What's in Arizona?"

"Survivalist compound," Pally replied. He took a sip of the little water bottle all the best Zyp drivers offered their riders. "I'm gonna hunker down with them, if they'll have me."

"Gum?"

"Wha?"

"Do you want some gum?" Farrow clarified, as she passed a small box, the kind one might see cigarette packs lined up in behind a bodega counter, filled with a panoply of gum types and flavors. Farrow, Pally was coming to realize, was far more than a 4.8 driver. 4.9, at *least*.

He considered the myriad options before him. There were too *many* options, really. Peppermint Blast? Arctic Freeze? Cinnamon Burn? One that just said Beet Root? There were at least a dozen others besides. God, how he hated myriad options; he liked two, *maybe* three options from which to make the wrong choice. "Um," he decided.

Farrow shrugged and withdrew the box. "Let me know if you change your mind."

That, Pally thought, *would require that I'd made it up to begin with.*

"I don't suppose there's any likelihood of you taking me all the way to Arizona, is there?"

Farrow emanated an aura of demurral. It was hardly necessary for her to say "unfortunately not, my friend. Fun as it would be to go on a little road trip adventure, I've got my own shit to worry about. I can give you two hours' worth of driving, at least. So you pick where you wanna go, a train station or a rental car joint or whatever, and as long as it's not more than about two hours' of driving away, I'll get you there."

Neither of those places sounded especially appealing; both required patience and stasis, either of which could prove fatal.

"Ah…" Pally's phone rang. He looked at it. Katie calling. Fuck, he should have called her as soon as he was in the car. She must have been worried sick. "I have to take this," he told Farrow, "just keep heading east for now, I'll figure out where to go in a second." He answered the phone. "Hi, honey."

"Are you alright?" she wondered with, *finally*, an appropriate amount of concern.

"I'm fine. I'm in a Zyp headed east. Sorry I didn't call you sooner, I was ju-"

"Don't worry about that. I can't imagine…oh, honey. This is really happening, isn't it?"

"…"

"Right, that sounds stupid. I get that. I guess I was just in some kind of, I don't know, shock or denial or something, even once the guy started shooting. It just didn't seem real, until…"

"Until what?! Is Lily hurt?"

"Oh! Oh, no. Nothing like that. I just meant, it didn't really seem real until, and this is going to sound silly, I know that, but it didn't seem real to me until the news crews came in and started asking me about it."

Pally smiled. "Yes, that does sound silly." He knew what she meant, though. Catching that glimpse of himself on the news, shot from the reassuringly familiar eye-in-the-sky vantage point, had given this endless nightmare a more comprehensible shape. It was like seeing a chaotic snarl of yarn knit itself, as if by magic, into a mitten with room for just a middle finger. "Just not as silly as you'd think. How'd you do?"

"In the interview?"

"Yeah."

"Well, I'm sure I was a fucking mess. I don't even remember what I said."

"Did they try to talk to Lily?"

"Tried. I didn't let them."

Pally nodded. "Can I talk to her?"

"Yeah. Patrick. Stay safe out there. If there's anything I can do to help, anybody I can call…"

"Thanks babe. I'll let you know."

"Please do. I love you."

"Love you too."

After some shuffling, Lily's voice came on the line: "Daddy?"

"Hey, sweetie."

"Daddy, don't die. That would be bad."

"I'll see what I can do," he joked. Only perhaps his delivery hadn't been as sharp as he'd imagined – or maybe it was *too* sharp – because as if at the flip of a switch, Lily was bawling into the receiver.

Just as suddenly, Pally was too.

16

"I'll pay for your gas."

Farrow shook her head. "I'm sorry, man. No can do."

"I'll give you five hundred dollars. Plus money to cover your gas on the way back."

She sighed and shot Pally a pitying look in the rearview.

"A thousand. Plus gas"

237

"I can't."

"What do you have to do that's more important than a thousand dollars plus gas?"

The eyes in the mirror weren't quite as pitying this time.

"Sorry. That didn't come out right. I just…" he fiddled with the electronic window openers set into the door. *Bvvvv*, down. *Bvvvv*, up. "I'm just trying to think strategically. Like, what's my next move? I gotta get a ride without waiting for it. If I just sit on my thumb at a bus stop, or a train station, somebody'll I'm sure start filming me, or a news crew'll splash me on the local five. Then Gun Guy sees it-"

"You're calling him Gun Guy?"

"It suits him."

Farrow laughed. "That's true enough."

"Anyway, you get what I'm saying. I'm sitting there eating Cheetos when I get a needle in my neck, then I'm dead. So…I just don't know what to do. Unless, you know…"

"I can't drive you the whole way. And you've still gotta pick where I *am* driving you, because we're coming right up on two hours."

"Do you mind if I ask what you do?"

"Depends on the tone you ask it in."

Pally smiled. "Let's say I used a nice one."

Farrow matched his grin. "Well, I'm all over the place, really. I run all the rideshare apps by day, which keeps me pretty well busy. Then in the evenings I'm either babysitting, tutoring or, very rarely, free. Bad news for you is, tonight's not a free night."

"Which is tonight?"

"Tutoring."

"You're turning down a grand plus gas for tutoring?"

"Hey man," Farrow chuckled, "ordinarily I'd agree, but we're talking SAT prep for the last shot at testing. Moneyed types up in the hills are willing to pay *crazy* amounts for tutors right now."

"How much?"

"Ah-ah, sorry Charlie, but bailing now would be a ding on my reputation I'm not interest in trying to buff out. But hey, why not just keep calling yourself Zyps? You've got a hell of a headstart on your Gun Guy. As long as you keep moving, you should be fine!"

"That sounds expensive."

"Says the guy who was trying to match crazy money."

"That's a very good point."

The two sat in silence for a minute. Then Pally got on his phone, opened up Westmore Maps, and asked "so how much longer do I have you for?"

17

Pally had Farrow drop him at a spot in Palm Springs that, on the Zyp app, seemed like it would have a lot of cars nearby and available. Naturally, by the time he arrived, all of the Zyp cars had zipped elsewhere.

"They're all gone," he told Farrow.

She sighed. "Ok, call one. I'll wait here with you.

Bullets start flying, you hop in and we're gone."

He smiled at her. "You're so much more than a 4.8."

Her face dropped. "I have a 4.8 rating? Oh, what the fuck!"

Pally debated saying sorry, but recognized the damage done and instead called himself another Zyp. While he waited, he changed the card on file from his debit to his credit; he could worry about it later. What was his credit limit? High enough, he thought, based on absolutely nothing.

Changing the payment info cancelled the ride he'd called, of course, so he called another.

"Gosh," he tried to cover, "these things do take their time."

"4.8," Farrow shook her head at the windshield. She turned to Pally. "See what I'm saying, about dings in reputation? That shit follows you."

Pally shivered and checked his phone. Three minutes away. He conveyed this to Farrow, who was too sore about her score to take much notice.

Finally the second Zyp, a Nissan Altima driven by *Raul*, who had 4.9 stars (for some reason, Pally felt it necessary to hold the phone just a bit closer to himself, and so further from Farrow), whose favorite drivin' tunes were *Creedence!!!* and who was from *Indio*, pulled up behind Farrow's Soul.

"Well," Pally said through the open door, "thanks for your help."

Farrow smiled and extended her hand, which Pally shook. "My pleasure. I'd say any time, but, well…"

"You've got shit to do."

Farrow made a finger gun at Pally and clicked her tongue. She had the good sense to immediately regret this decision, mumbling "sorry" as Pally mumbled "no worries" and shut the door.

As the Soul puttered off, Pally piled into the Altima's backseat. He asked "Raul?", as everyone who has ever used a ridesharing app knows that the only acceptable greeting is to ask the driver their name, straightaway, no matter what.

"Yeah. Patrick?" Raul returned. This guy knew what was up. A little too well, unfortunately: he, as Farrow had before him, turned to Pally, went a bit slack around the jaw, and asked Pally if he was "the guy from the thing".

This was a pattern that would repeat itself throughout the night. Raul proved to be even less gung-ho than Farrow had been, taking him only as far as Coachella (the town – apparently Pally had narrowly missed the concert thing they had there, thank goodness). Raul dropped Pally off at a rather dismal, dark corner that even the brilliant setting sun couldn't touch, then fucked right off into said sunset. Funnily enough, Pally was mad about this. Farrow had spoiled him, as far as Zyp drivers went, and here he was coming to expect similar kindnesses from everybody, only to be annoyed when they failed to deliver. But was that an unreasonable expectation to have of a 4.9? Certainly not!

After what felt like an eternity (though the clock on his phone that was giving him the 'low battery' alert, damnit, anyway, the phone insisted it had only been seven minutes), the next Zyp pulled up. It was driven by *Chad* (drivin' tunes *what ever*, from *my momma*). As might be expected from his supplied answers, Chad only had 4.6 stars, ordinarily a cancellable offence. But having first-hand knowledge of how reputation dings can happen to good people, and also being chased by a professional assassin, put Pally in a charitable mood.

He got into the car, which was a bong on wheels. There was another smell in there, something like burnt plastic, only sweeter. Not a pleasant kind of sweet. He very nearly ducked out, but thought better of it, and was ultimately happy he did: Chad was a brusque but well-meaning fella, so big he was practically doing yoga just to fit in the front seat. Put it this way, if it emerged that Chad was powering his Honda Accord the way the Flintstones powered their cars, Pally would not have been shocked. Nor was Chad an exceptional conversationalist. He wasn't rude, just…well, he wasn't quite locked in to the wavelength of regular verbal intercourse. Just as a for instance, when Pally said "Chad?" upon entering the car, Chad replied "I know, right?" Not *so* far outside the bounds of acceptability, but…a *little* bit outside, yeah. When Pally asked him if he'd ever been to that Coachella festival, Chad replied "Wednesday." And so it went.

Where it went was right on down the 10 as far as Blythe, on the California/Arizona border. Chad was insistent about dropping him off there on the Cali side, which Pally tried hard not to imagine was related to some kind of parole agreement. Blythe was tiny, but fortunately had a few hotels. Pally called another Zyp and headed inside the lobby of a Hampton Inn to get out of the early evening heat.

He regretted it instantly.

Within thirty seconds, he had three phones trained on him. The concierge emerged from behind the desk to pepper Pally with questions, none of them in any way specific. "So what's it like?" was the closest they came to answerable. By the time the Zyp arrived (*Bethany*, 4.9, *I'll listen to just about anything, Chicago*) Pally could hear one of the phone-wielders shrieking "OH BOY! They're using my footage!" Which, first of all, who actually shouts *oh boy* when they're excited? And second of all, Pally mulled in the background of his mind as he clambered into the back of the Nissan Pathfinder and said "Bethany?", *shit*. Because the *they* that person was shrieking about was the news. Pally checked his phone that had eleven percent battery left, *shit again*, and sure enough there he was on the news. *Flying Through Blythe* was the headline, accompanied by a rather dimwitted close-up of Pally's face. Ok, so it was the face that was dimwitted. *His* face. But cinematic though Tort-Oil was ensuring this venture was, there wasn't exactly a hair and makeup trailer to which he could retire between takes.

"Excuse me," Pally asked Bethany, "do you have a charger I could use for just a bit?"

Bethany turned all the way around to look at Pally, as they were merging onto the highway. *This was a 4.9?!*

"What kind of phone?" she wondered as though they weren't hurtling blindly down the road at sixty miles per hour.

"Eyesontheroadpl-"

"Huh?"

"iPhone!"

"Sure!" She turned back around (thank goodness), flipped open a little cubbyhole on her center console, and started rooting around (oh goodness). Thankfully, she found the charger in short order, plugged it into the cigarette lighter and passed it back.

"Thank you," Pally tried to say. His throat was awfully dry all of a sudden, though. "Thanks," he managed more forcefully. He punched the address of the survivalist compound into Zyp on his phone, which caused Bethany's phone to *ding*. It was another three hours' drive, but, well, maybe Bethany would prove to be a true 4.9er after all. "Is there any way you can get me all the way there?"

Bethany studied her phone, swiped her finger along the screen to trace the journey, zooming in and out, tutting and cocking her head from side to side, all while they were zooming down the highway, and it was nighttime, and maybe you should or could focus a little more carefully on the road, unless you're the killer Tort-Oil sent after me, unless Gun Guy was just a goof and a flimflam to get me into this car as you drive it off a bridge and oh shit Pally realized he'd been saying a certain amount of that out loud but wasn't sure which parts he had, but those eyes glaring at him in the rearview made it seem like the answer was probably *all of it*.

"Sorry," he added.

Bethany shrugged and said "I want two hundred bucks tip."

Two hundred? A steal! "Ok," Pally agreed.

"Cash. Now."

Pally frowned. "I don't have cash."

"You have Venmo?"

"...that sounds like a personal question."

"No, it's an app. It lets you send money."

"Oh. No."

So Bethany talked Pally through getting Venmo, which he did, and promptly sent her two hundred smackeroos. He knew she got the money because she spent *forever* scrutizing the transaction on her phone.

"Ok?" he asked her.

"Ok," she smiled.

"Ok." Pally sighed. Good lord, he was tired. *Exhausted*, even. It was nearly tomorrow, and on top of that, riding in cars always made him drowsy. It was like being rocked to sleep by a Transformer. "Do you usually drive this late?"

"Always."

"I'm not usually up this late." Pally yawned. "I'm gonna rest my eyes for a minute, is that alright?"

Bethany smiled into the mirror. She had a pretty smile, which probably accounted for the lion's share of her score. "I transferred the cash to my bank account, so you do whatever the hell you want back there. *Not literally*," she added hastily.

Pally nodded his appreciation, curled up against the window, and had just enough time to think *boy, good thing I'm with a 4.9er, or I wouldn't feel safe doing this* before he was plunged into a dreamless sea of night.

18

He awoke to stars, twinkling in the twilight.

Oh fuck.

Aliens, shining lights in the...

No...

Worse.

News teams.

Pally looked in the front seat, but Bethany was outside the car, being interviewed by one crew and circled by three others. Meanwhile, there were no fewer than seven crews jostling for shots in through the various windows.

Turning to the passengerside of the car, Pally glanced out the rear window and made eye contact with one of the reporters, who looked like he'd just clocked out of being a mannequin at Men's Wearhouse. The man hopped an inch off the ground, waved his crew over, then rapped on the window with his knuckle.

Thum thum thum.

"Mr. Hollen!" he shouted through the glass. "Toby Callender, Live-Witness News Action Team Six at Five." He snapped each word off with his teeth. "I have just a few questions for you regarding your experience as a bold new vision of and for entertainment!"

Thum thum thum from the rear driverside window. Pally whipped around to find a pantsuit that looked less-than-pleased to have a woman in it. "Mr. Hollen!" she boomed. "Nancy Myers-Briggs, no relation, Action News Accuweather Team Trust Fall Fifteeen on the Twos. When you entered the contest for the gas, why?"

THUM from directly above Pally. He looked up to see a human form crawling along the roof of the car. A face peered in through the sunroof, its features obliterated by the tinting of the glass. It looked disturbingly like Mr. Silhouette, from the Tort-Oil informational video. "Mr. Hollen!" the person-shaped hole in the fabric of reality roared. "Dan Glimp, Glimp's Pix with an X, Wha-"

"Don't talk to him!" both Toby Callender and Nancy Myers-Briggs screamed. "He's a blogger! He's not a real journalist!"

"The real journalist is the one who gets the scoop!" Dan fired back.

That set off what must have passed for a brawl with these folks, i.e. waving their fingers so hard that their hair came slightly uncemented. Pally tuned it out, though. He turned on his phone, glaring angrily at the white apple that filled the screen for longer and longer every time he updated the damn thing.

Finally, the menu appeared. Pally slapped through to the map and grimaced.

Fuck. They were close to the survivalist camp. *Very* close. Like, an hour's brisk walk kind of close.

In a sense, that was good news. He didn't exactly feel

rested after his two-odd hours of shuteye, but he was confident that he had enough, ha, ha, gas in the tank to hoof it to the camp.

The bad news, of course, was that there wasn't much else out this way, or indeed much reason to be out here in the first place, if not to go visit Brimley Furlough and his goofball buddies at Desert Island.

And that he was out here was about to be all over the airwaves, if it wasn't already. Which Gun Guy would no doubt see. And, being the professional he was, he would no doubt connect the dots and know precisely where Pally was heading.

He'd counted on being caught out eventually; such was his luck. He just hadn't anticipated it happening within literally twenty-four hours.

Why, oh why couldn't Bethany, who was going to be getting a one star rating on Zyp for *certain*, have pulled this shit closer to a town, or at some sort of junction even? A dirt crossroads? That would have at least had some fun parallels with American mythology, the story about the guy who sold his soul to The Guy to get the thing. A new guitar? Something. Didn't matter, because now Pally was the new Guy who had sold his soul to get the thing. Pally was the new American myth.

That was the point. Didn't matter. There was no point to it, wondering why or why not. This was what was happening. The sooner he got to that survivalist camp, the safer he'd be.

Assuming they took him in at all. Which had been an outside shot to begin with. But if he showed up trailing half of Arizona's local news teams? He couldn't imagine that helping his case.

So how to get rid of them?

He checked the ignition of the car, but Bethany had taken the key. Clever.

Pally sighed and did a quick three-sixty in his seat. Surrounded. This must be what the last lobster in the grocery store tank feels like. Lobsters were supposed to be pretty smart, right? That's why he was supposed to consider them? Well, then Pally needed to think like a lobster.

What would a lobster do right now? WWLD? Probably sit in the tank and wait for death. So thinking like a lobster was a dead end. Rats.

Say, weren't rats supposed to be pretty smart? WWRD? Probably something devious.

Now *there* was a useful idea.

Pally looked out the rear window of the car. Relatively clear, just a lone boom op and a cameraman's shoulder in the way. Quick as his modest girth would allow, Pally reached to the dashboard and punched the button that popped the rear hatch. Only, seeing as this was a new car, the hatch-pop button didn't stop at popping. Modern automobiles spared their drivers the onerous task of, ugh, physically *opening* the gate with their *hands*. So the Pathfinder automatically whirred its hatch open, a task accompanied by a loud *BEEP BEEP BEEP*ing.

The *BEEP*s were as good as chum; the news crews whipped themselves into a frenzy, shouting and jostling and converging upon the slowly rising gate of the car, oblivious to the Pally-shaped shadow slipping out the front passengerside door and skittering into the pitch-black of the desert.

He probably made it about two hundred feet before he heard somebody shout "THERE HE IS!", which was further than he'd expected to get.

19

Unforgiving spotlights, apparently designed to make the subjects upon whom they are trained look fatally ill, swung on Pally, illuminating the landscape before him save the slice of his long, many-tendriled shadow.

Lucky they swept around when they did; Pally saw the foot-deep gully with just enough time to leap over it. Had he not seen it, that would have been a broken ankle for sure. No doubt that would have proven fatal in short order.

This was what he'd expected. He hadn't for one second imagined he would give them the slip without a bit of a chase. But he *also* hadn't imagined it would be this hard. In movies, when somebody's in the desert at night, it just looks like a really cloudy day, everything coated in a deep, dark blue. But you can still see.

There was nothing to see here. Beyond the reach of the camera's lights, the sands became void. The boundary was unnervingly sharp, even as its dimensions bubbled and boiled with each stride the cameramen made behind him. It was like some protean cliff's edge skirting an abyss of untold depth – if, indeed, there was any bottom at all.

What made it all the more disturbing was that the abyss was precisely where Pally needed to be. Yet the cliff continued to assemble itself before him, forever out of reach, leading him through a darkness that made orientation impossible.

Pally considered, in all seriousness, that he may have fallen asleep in the back of the Pathfinder, and was now having a nightmare. Scratch that – this was definitely a nightmare, no question about that. All that remained to be determined was whether or not he was sleeping.

No, there was one other thing to determine: why was he still running in a straight line? Weren't you supposed to zig-zag when you were being shot at? That seemed like something he'd heard somewhere. Probably on TV. Ha, ha.

Pally zigged to his right. He heard some of the digital shooters behind him shout, watched a few of the lights forging his path shudder and vanish. Somebody – a few somebodies – had tripped. Good.

Bad: by temporarily slipping out of their line of sight, he was hurtling headlong into blindness. He could hear his feet crunching across the rocks and sand, feel the dry wind scratching at his chin stubble, taste the copper from within and grit from without.

Still shrouded, he zigged right again before the lights had a chance to find him. He was heading back the way he'd come from now, on a parallel track. This was his gamble – he could only hope the news crews wouldn't expect something so idiotic and counterintuitive. If they came upon the idea when he failed to materialize in front of them, as they very likely would…well, Pally could only hope he'd have found a place to hide by then.

Easier said than done. As long as darkness reigned, *everywhere* was a hiding place. How could he know what was hiding him from sight if there was no sight from which to hide? It wasn't hard to imagine crouching down behind a rock and giggling about his good fortune, only to be blinded by fluorescence and peppered with questions in the very next instant.

Nothing to it but to do it, though. That was also something he'd probably heard on TV.

He zagged left, putting more distance between himself and his pursuers on a perpendicular track. The ground beneath his feet was getting softer, shifting beneath each step, robbing him of precious velocity. Breath was beginning to cost him blood, it seemed. Each gasping inhale was a dagger in his lungs, each exhale brought him closer to incontinence.

Just as he was considering turning back and returning to more stable foundations, he felt the sands rising. He was scaling a hill.

Ok! A hill might just do it!

A look over his shoulder brought a strange sight: the news crews had realized that they were no longer on his trail, but as yet hadn't fanned out to search for him. No doubt, none wanted to leave the others unattended, for fear that another should discover him, and so net the scoop of the day, without the others' having their cameras at the ready. It was like peering through a microscope and seeing a single-celled organism with poor proprioception trying to play duck-duck-goose with its far edges.

For a moment, Pally lost his sense of perspective, and with it his equilibrium. He teetered and very nearly tumbled back down the hill, but found balance by closing his eyes. Save the blonde amoeba vanishing from sight, eyes shut was functionally indistinguishable from eyes open. That was enough to ground him.

Eyes still shut, he turned around and opened them. Pure dark. Ah, that was better.

But not *pure* dark, though; it was only now, as he bent over and recruited his hands to help him scramble the rest of the way up the rise, that he was able to appreciate the beauty of the wasteland. It was true that he lived in a desert, but only in a technical sense. Los Angeles was its own unique ecosystem, its climate dictated by a monthly bill. One was most often in a building or a car, only venturing outside for a substantial amount of time if one had a location shoot or in the event of an emergency, the former often occasioning the latter (union training manuals would be greatly enhanced by a passage on heat stroke, say no more). It was simple, in some ways inevitable, to forget that LA existed by sheer force of will. Any day now, it would run out of water, and barring another Owens Valley to rape (or another Roman Polanski to make a movie about it, which was a match made in hell when you thought about it), the city of angels would crumble and blow away in a matter of days. How many people in that city had genuinely useful skills? Pally knew all about voltages and amps, but if the wall socket had no power, or the generator had no fuel (and the Tort-Oil stations were shuttered, thus rendering his card useless), what could he bring to the table in terms of survival skills?

Pally quickly realized that his mind was off on this tangent as a way of subtly broaching a topic that would occasion far more panic. Fuck the hypothetical collapse of Los Angeles – how was Pally going to survive *here*?

He realized he'd scaled the hill when he lifted his right foot and couldn't find the ground to drive it down into. Instead it barreled through nothing and kept on going. A yelp nearly escaped Pally's throat, but he managed to stifle it in the nick of time. The cost of that vocal discretion was a lapse in his ambulatory attentions. His right foot grew three times its usual weight, dragging the rest of him along for the ride as it plummeted down the far side of the hill.

The sand was soft, at least. "At least" recurred in a different tone of voice after he'd managed four ass-over-end tumbles, though, as in: at least, the sand was soft *near the top of the hill.*

At the *bottom* of the hill, which is traditionally where one lands when rolling down an incline, was a bed of rocks and cacti and, judging by feel, used needles and rusty playground equipment.

Pally peeled himself from the spines and stones,

remembering how bad his neck wound had felt in contrast to how bad it had actually been and using that to reassure himself that, no, his back and shoulders and head and legs probably weren't *nearly* as wrecked as they felt.

His lone consolation was that he had made it, given himself to the tides of night and been pulled from his pursuers. He was cold and bleeding and sweaty and probably broken in not a few important places, had no clue how he was going to stay alive if he couldn't manage to find the survivalists in short order, couldn't even *consider* what would happen if they didn't take him in... and yet, chilling though all of that was, he was warmed by his triumph.

Metaphorically. More literally, he was freezing his ass off. As he heard distant shouts of frustration, car and van engines rumbling to life and then fading away, Pally's smile chattered. Then that, too, faded away, without the benefit of an echo.

20

He didn't know what was more shocking – that he'd fallen asleep freezing and woken up baking, or that he'd managed to get to sleep at all.

Pushing himself upright, Pally took stock of the wounds he could see, and was pleased to receive confirmation that, on the whole, they were not as bad as they'd felt. He had a pretty nasty gash along his left tricep, and both of his ankles felt sprained, but he'd be able to limp to the survivalists, he thought.

Assuming.

He stuffed his hand into his pocket, fully expecting to find his phone missing or broken or dead, in which case he would be too. Remarkably, it was still there, and even more remarkably, it still worked, and even *more* remarkably, he had three bars of signal.

It was humbling to recognize that, had this little gizmo in his hand failed to pull through in any sense, or had he been unable to plug it into a little wire in Bethany the 1-star Traitor's car, his story would very likely end here in the not-so-flats of Arizona, and Tort-Oil's cat-and-mouse documentary would become an unsolved mystery piece. Which they might have loved even more, come to think of it.

Pally hoped so. He was only too happy to disappoint them.

He thumbed up the survivalists on the map. Still about an hour's brisk walk. A little more, now – it seemed he'd made his escape in the opposite direction of the one he ought to have been going in. Yep, that was more like it, re: his luck.

It was a stroke of good fortune, though, that he had this hill to orient him in some capacity. Keeping his eye on the map, watching the little blue dot and, more importantly, the little flashlight beam it emitted to specify which direction the dot was headed (a feature that never ceased to both astonish and disturb Pally), he began his trek back up the hill.

An image of news vans prowling the basin by day,

unwilling or unable to accept their quarry's escape, struck him with such force that as he crested the rise, he actual *saw* their satellite dishes and rotini antennae. He gasped, and the mirage vanished. Still, fear counseled caution; he peeked over top the hill slowly, carefully.

Nothing. Nobody. Just desert, far as the eye could see. Or rather, for as long as the eye could look before it filled up with sand.

He checked the map. Headed the right way, facing the right way. Ok. Ok. Time to get moving; this being the spot of Pally's last sighting, Gun Guy was no doubt on his way here at this very moment. Quickly as he could without losing his footing in the ever-shifting sand, Pally descended the slope and followed his little blue flashlight beam.

21

The walk to the camp was rather long and eventful. Being exhausted from what, for Pally, constituted a month's worth of physical exertion all expended at once, a brisk walking pace was more than he could manage. So the journey to the Desert Island compound took him nearer to three hours, factoring in the time he spend marveling (from a considerable distance) at the scorpions, snakes, and probably less fatal meerkat-looking things he saw along the way. Were there meerkats in America? Outside of zoos? He couldn't remember. He didn't think so. It didn't matter. But he didn't think so.

As he neared the spot on the map which corresponded to the spot on the planet that the survivalists called home, he realized that he didn't actually know what he was looking for. For all the videos and photos he'd seen on their website, none of them showed any sort of identifying frontage. The reasons were fairly obvious, but as he approached the pin on the map and saw nothing of note, not even the fenced-in bits they'd shown on their website, he started to get worried. What if they'd closed up shop, and forgotten to update their website? That didn't seem like a very survivalist thing to do, but stranger things had happened, and they tended to happen to Pally.

Worst-case scenario, he figured, he could call for help. That would tip off Gun Guy, and put Pally in quite a bit of danger…but if there was nobody out here, he might not have any other choice.

That defeatist train of thought was derailed when Pally realized that, no, he was in exactly the right place. He knew he'd found Desert Island when three guys in desert brush ghillie suits with tan-painted assault rifles popped up and started screaming. It was an angry alphabet soup they spouted, but Pally could make out a word here or there, words like "halt" and "trespassing" and "liberty".

"Wait!" Pally cried, raising his palms in the air. "I need help! I want to join you!"

Two of the dusty Cousin Its fell silent. The other squeezed off a last "…Founding Fathers!" before he, too, lapsed into quietude.

"I'm in a bit of a predicament. A pickle," Pally clar-ified. "And I w-"

"Hey!" the ghillie on the left exclaimed. "You're that guy from the thing, ain'tcha?"

Still smarting from Bethany's betrayal, Pally's first instinct was to say 'no'. But these guys probably didn't pose the same risk as she had, right? The chances of them calling up news crews and telling them to *come on over* were pretty slim. Besides, judging by the facilities he'd seen online, these guys weren't hurting for cash. Pally had to imagine the moolah was why Bethany had double-dealt him like that.

Then there was the most obvious disincentive to dishonesty: these guys could catch Pally out on a lie in literally three seconds. Honestly, at this point one could probably search "the guy from the thing" and have one's screen sullied with Pally's picture.

He shuddered to consider which picture of him they would use. No doubt, it would not be a flattering one. Assuming such a photo of him even existed.

"Yes," he admitted, "I'm the guy from the thing."

All three of the men before him lifted their masks to reveal genial faces with bright smiles. They knew who he was. Which was unnerving, but on the plus side, it meant he wouldn't have to go through the humiliating experience of explaining the entire situation to them. What would he even say? *I won a contest for free gas but didn't read the rules, which included a hitman trying to kill me for a year?* How could he say that and *not* feel like a complete-

"Wait," asked the guy in the middle, who as it happened was Brimley Furlough, "what thing are we talkin' about?"

Ugh.

22

Pally and his three survivalist guides piled into a golf cart "hidden" nearby beneath a gargantuan pile of tumbleweeds (the towering bramble put Pally in mind of a bear trying to hide behind a thin curtain). Brenda, the smallest of the welcoming committee, hoped Pally enjoyed his ride in the Desert Island Limo. Then she chuckled, which was how Pally knew that was supposed to be funny.

As they puttered deeper into the desert, Pally brought Brimley up to speed. Brenda and Washington, the one who had initially recognized Pally as the guy from the thing, knew all about what kind of pickle Pally was in. But Brimley quite literally lived under a rock, and so it was the work of the entire ride to the compound proper to bring him up to speed.

At the end of the explanation, Brimley looked at Pally as he might a spider he'd intended to squash, until noticing it was doing an eight-legged softshoe routine on the kitchen counter. "Guess you learned a lesson about the little prints," was all he had to offer.

"To say the least," Pally replied.

Brimley looked at Brenda, then at Washington, then at the ground rushing past, at which he shook his head disapprovingly. "That's how they getcha. Take an honest man, don't expect much from the world save a bit of honesty in return, and getchim with the little prints." He looked at Pally, his expression inscrutable. "You wanna crash for a year?"

"I mean…I hope I'm not crashing, but yeah."

Brimley's fuzzy face ballooned into a friendly grin. "Turn of the words, to say crashin'. Naw, we got all kinds of room. Just lost a few heads to the grind, didn't we?" He looked to his two compatriots for confirmation.

"Sure did," Washington averred.

"Scott took a job in Phoenix, can you believe it?" Brenda asked of Pally.

"I…" *guess it depends on the job* was what Pally thought, but as that wasn't the response that was being solicited, he went with "…can't. I can't believe Scott would do that."

"Phoenix!" Brenda marveled.

"Phoenix," Washington mourned.

"So it goes," Brimley shrugged. He heaved himself out of the golf cart before it had fully come to a halt, prompting Brenda and Washington to follow suit. "We keep outside contact to a minimal," he explained to Pally, "for a host of whys. Chief among 'em is the temptation. Gettin' ends together on Desert Island ain't always a picnic, I'll tell you up top, we ain't got little prints here. It ain't always a picnic, is it?"

"Sure ain't," Brenda agreed.

"Sometimes, but not all times," Washington blueskyed.

Brimley nodded as he approached the massive chainlink perimeter fence. It was massive, had to be at least fifteen feet tall, with barbed wire corkscrewing along the summit in thick, overlapping snarls. Ordinarily, this sort of thing would have creeped Pally out. But now, given the circumstances, he just smiled. Let Gun Guy come for him. Just let him try.

It did cross his mind, as Brimley jammed a key into a rusty padlock so huge it looked like a Halloween decoration, that if the Desert Island gang were anything less than one hundred percent on the up and up, Pally could be walking into an even bigger pickle than the one in which he currently found himself. Perhaps it was that cinematic lens by which he found himself imprisoned, but this looked like the part of the movie where sinister music starts playing. The helpful yokels turn out to be less than helpful, that was practically its own genre.

The more he thought about it, the uneasier he became. His reservations grew as he stepped through the gate and listened to Brimley lock it back up behind him – the scrape of the key along the lockface as it sought the hole, the clicking of the teeth as they slotted into the locking mechanism, the crack of the shackle as Brimley slammed it home again.

Before he knew it, Pally was approaching a kind of nervous hysteria. He still didn't believe they would turn him over to the news vultures for a quick buck – but he'd failed to consider there were worse fates that could befall him. He couldn't as yet imagine what those might be, but that was why they were scary; they were quite literally unimaginable.

Yet he continued to follow the Islanders, through a heavy iron door set into a crooked, steel-reinforced barn-looking structure. The door itself had one of those whirly-wheels on it, like it had been cadged from a Soviet submarine. Brimley spun the wheel and heaved the door open, standing back to let his friends and new guest lead the way. It was a homely gesture made sinister by Pally's own suspicions.

This is stupid. Those three words hummed in Pally's head like a marquee: THIS IS STUPID. Too bad he didn't know to what they were referring. Was it his paranoia that was stupid, or his blindly following strangers, *well-armed* strangers, into an underground bunker, after having gone to great lengths to ensure that nobody knew where he was? The news crews had an idea, but if he vanished…well, his wife knew where he was, but she was fully expecting him to fall off the map for a while. Which…

…Gun Guy wouldn't go after her, would he? Surely that was against the rules?

Ha! Rules. What were the rules here?

(THIS IS STUPID)

WHAT? *What* was stupid? That wasn't helpful, that free-floating roast in search of a target.

Say it was his continued acquiescence to these folks' eager hospitality. Was it stupid that he was continuing to follow them down these clanging grate stairs, clutching a cold handrail fashioned from just the kinds of lead pipes that, as far as movies were concerned, existed solely to cave people's skulls in? He wanted to leave, he wanted to turn around and run screaming at the locked door, kicking at it until either somebody opened it, or, or…well, he didn't know what. But he didn't turn and scream and kick, not because he was afraid of being bopped in the nose or thrown down the stairs or whatever – at least then he'd know where he stood (or fell) here. No, he didn't do it because he was afraid of being rude.

Ah. Was this it? Was this what was stupid? Wasn't this what had gotten him into this situation to begin with? Julia had given him just the sort of dire warning he ought to have recognized. In fact he *had* appreciated it for the dark omen that it was. Yet he signed the papers anyway, despite not knowing what was on them, despite being warned that he *ought* to. Why? Why did he do that? Because it would have been awkward not to. Because his damned agreeability had gotten the best of him.

Not anymore, he resolved. No longer would he be Pally the Yes Man. It was time to be a No Man! He wasn't comfortable here, he didn't feel safe in the least, and for once he was going to raise his voice and speak his mind! Any second now, he would confidently assert himself, tell Brimley not to open this second whirly-wheel door deep underground, demand that he be released back into the wilds of Arizona, where a man could be certain of his place in the world, even if that place was not a great one. Yes, it was really bound to happen without a moment's notice, he would s-

"You ok?" Brenda asked.

"Oh, yeah," Pally shrugged. Goddamnit!

Brimley turned and studied Pally. "You look worried, bud."

Pally bit his tongue, took a deep breath, and managed to squeeze "actually, a little" out of his face.

"Hm. Ah!" Brimley's face lit up as he reached to the back of his waistline and withdrew a handgun.

Somewhere, a young girl shrieked. Pally realized only a moment later that the young girl was he.

Brimley started slightly, then grinned, spun the gun on the finger he had stuffed in the trigger guard (which seemed *super dangerous*), and handed the whole thing to Pally, butt-first. "Safety's on, but it's loaded, so keep care with it. Soon as after lunch, we can start teachin' ya to shoot, if that'd save ya some sweat."

The phrase *Hollywood liberal* was often used derogatorily by most of the country, an epithet interchangeable with *bleeding-heart liberal*. To Pally, though, *Hollywood liberal* meant something specific, particularly as pertained to guns: a firm conviction that guns were, broadly speaking, bad…yet just as firm a conviction that they were fucking *awesome*. Like most of his friends, Pally genuinely despaired over every report of gun violence: police shootings and school shootings and post office shootings, the list seemed endless. He favored the strictest gun control measures possible, age restrictions, background checks, cavity searches, whatever it took to screen out those who couldn't be trusted with a firearm from those who could.

But golly, *John Wick* was fucking *awesome*. An hour and forty minutes of Keanu Reeves shooting the entire world in the face. What made Pally uncomfortable about this was how comfortable he was with it. The cognitive dissonance only set in after the credits rolled; while the movie was going, Pally could hardly restrain himself from clapping and bouncing as his boy Neo shot more fools than the dipshit photographer at his and Katie's wedding. There were plenty of defenses he had prepared in his mind, should anybody ever challenge him on this (*it's more about the choreography than the shooting itself* was, he felt, his strongest), but much as he believed his justifications, they all seemed to have something hollow at the center. Like a hollow-point bullet, that when Keanu shot it at a guy, it would make his head blow up like ker-*SPLAT*, all over the wall, it'd be so fucking cool. But if it happened in real life, it'd be bad.

Such was the plight of the Hollywood liberal. Now, being handed a gun of his own, Pally felt such a surge of contradictory impulses – a natural distaste for guns, a desire to have some kind of protection here, a fear that the gun wasn't loaded and this was some kind of test, a desire to impress his hosts, a need to acquiesce in all things, a concern that perhaps he might fire a gun and like it a bit *too* much, and so on – the only comprehensible course of action his mind could fix upon was to slap the gun out of Brimley's hand and sprint, gibbering and full-tilt, into the wall. If he was lucky, he'd send his nose back into his brain or something, which would have been a *classic* Wick move.

Instead, Pally set aside the vanity that naturally attends self-consciousness and simply closed his eyes. He visualized each of his often mutually exclusive instincts as a cord, wound and knotted through itself. He imagined his own two hands as they were ten years ago reaching in to the Gordian tangle, tugging and pushing and pulling, liberating each strand from the others. He heard Brimley and the other two mumbling to each other, asking him if he was alright, asking him what was wrong, but he tuned them out, instead focusing on the task at imaginary hand.

Once the mess was sorted, he listened to the hum of each cord to find the most soothing note. Which sang to him most honestly? Which cords stretched from his heart, from the truest part of himself, and which were emissaries of his fearful, self-sabotaging mind?

Ah. This one.

Pally opened his eyes, his breath calmer and his heart rate more lax. He sighed and smiled.

"That's alright," he told Brimley in a voice that sounded an octave deeper than usual. "I can help out with other stuff, if that's alright with you."

Brimley looked at the gun in his hand as though for a moment, he considered that he might have handed Pally a shoehorn or a zucchini by accident. "It's a gun," he marveled. He looked almost pleadingly at Pally. "You don't want a gun?"

"No thank you," Pally replied.

"It's so you can feel safe," Brenda explained.

"Like a security blankie," Washington added, "only cooler."

"How many times I told you, don't compare it to a blankie!"

Washington shrugged. "I calls 'em like I sees 'em."

Brimley squinted at Pally as though concerned he had just invited little print incarnate into his bunker. "What other skills you got?"

"Electrical, mostly," Pally replied. "And I can get you as much gas as you could ever want, for free. Do you have generators that run on gas, I assume?"

His three hosts made the same De Niro horseshoe shape with their mouths and nodded.

"You're an odd duck," Brenda observed, "following strangers got high-powered weaponry in their hands into an underground bunker."

Pally shrugged. "I don't know if it's any odder than you inviting a stranger with a contract killer on his tail into your home."

"Aw, you ain't a stranger," Washington smiled. "We seen you on the TV."

23

The most remarkable thing about the Desert Island survivalists, the ranks of which ran to only nine members (ten including Pally), was how normal they were. Pally had expected kooks, but with the exception of a few minor quirks (one fella named Stan would only talk to you if there was about five feet of separation; Yolanda ended every conversation by saying "have a good night", regardless of the time of day), they were completely normal individuals who could be quite articulate about the fears that had driven them underground. None seemed to be reciting a party line, and Pally chalked the overlap between their stated concerns and those listed on the website as a case of the latter being dictated by the former, rather than vice versa. They were also, Pally marveled, far from objectivist nutjobs; they were some of the kindest, most generous people he had ever encountered. Were they not an indeterminate distance beneath the surface of the Arizona desert, it would have felt like a sleepaway camp for grownups.

A sleepaway camp would have had more to do, though. While the Islanders were off shooting or hunting or checking fences or whatever it was they did, Pally was left to free range around the facility, which best as he could tell was some kind of converted nuclear bunker (this he intuited from one of the closets in the main hall, which had a faded sticker explaining how best to don a hazmat suit). There were no sinister locked rooms, or straight-lipped warnings to not go down *this hall*. Brimley did advise him not to go into anybody's bunkroom without permission, given how tetchy these folks could get about the sanctity of what was *theirs*, but that was a commonsense injunction.

Pally looked high and low for something he could

do, some way he could contribute to the quality of life at Desert Island. Their electrical systems, which stemmed from a gas-powered generator (though there was indeed a handcrank backup), were admittedly beyond Pally's prowess. Far as he could tell, though, they looked good. He did help them get their surround sound set up in the living room, as before they'd had only the front speakers and the subwoofers wired up properly. They seemed quite appreciative of *that*, and the triumph was celebrated with a screening of *The Departed* on glorious HD-DVD (which just went to show, it really was impossible to prepare for *every* disaster). Pally offered to shell out for a Blu-Ray player, if only someone else could go get it. Brimley demurred, insisting the devices had gotten "too intelligent". He wasn't wrong, Pally granted.

So he ate their food (mostly dry and from buckets), drank their water (filtered and purified, Pally refused to ask from what), enjoyed their company, and reveled in the safety they provided him. For weeks, he waited for the catch, the little print that Brimley had so adamantly decried. The man was as good as his word, though; the gotcha never came. After about a month and a half, with the stir crazies setting in and not a peep from Gun Guy, Pally began to consider venturing topside for the first time since his arrival. Brimely quickly assembled the entirety of the Island to accompany him up, his own Praetorian guard. Groundward they shuffled, around the compound they meandered, and back down they went. It felt good to be in the fresh air, dry though it might have been.

Just before Pally's second month at Desert Island, Brimley hit him up for the gas card. The generator was running low, it seemed, and their stockpiles were dwindling. Pally happily handed over the card, and helped them carry the seven empty jugs up the stairs and out the door. Jugs didn't really cut it – these weren't those cute little red plastic cans with yellow spouts. They were just shy of being barrels, big, steel, industrial monsters, like a half-squat Walter White might fill with acid to dispose of a body. Even without gas in them, they were heavy. Getting them back down the stairs was not going to be fun. Unless they could just roll them down. That might be fun.

Four of the Desert Islanders left for the gas station. Brimley went with them – he never sent a man or woman out into "the field", as he called it, if he himself was not willing to go. That was Brimley's quirk, Pally supposed; he genuinely believed that the collapse of society could come at any moment, even when he was popping out to the Tort-Oil for some gas. Granted, the end had to come at *some* moment, and presumably *somebody* would be popping out to the Tort-Oil for some gas when it came, so it wasn't such a ridiculous con-cern, Pally supposed. Perhaps it was just spending months underground among the eschatologically mind-ed, but their gloomy prognostications seemed more and more plausible every day.

Among the Islanders who stayed behind was a younger couple, named Saul and Margot. So enamored were they of each other that Pally hadn't yet had much opportunity to speak with them, though a lack of desire was equally to blame. They put him in mind of his own domestic once-upon-a-time bliss with Katie, whom he missed more than he thought possible. He scarcely managed three or fours hours without taking out his phone and looking at photos or videos of her and Lily. There was internet down here, so Pally was able to Westmore Chat with them a few times, but a blurry, pixelated facsimile was no substitute for the real thing. On their first call, they couldn't stop saying how much they missed each other. From the second on, they never said it; it didn't need saying, and only took time from more important topics.

Such as: Lily had won the science fair with a baking soda volcano that erupted in "a million billion colors". Such as: Katie, who had taken up yoga a year or two ago, had done her first full handstand (though she blanched when Pally needled her to prove it). Such as: Gun Guy had not shown his face around the house or the neighborhood, thank goodness. Such as: Katie had recruited a delightfully game Lily in a misinformation campaign, coaching her daughter to go to school and "let slip" that Daddy was in Seattle, now outside Salt Lake City (there were all sorts of doomsday preppers amongst the Mormons, so that was the most plausible) now all the way over in Boston. Some of Lily's friends, in turn, took the misinformation to their parents, who took it to the news in hopes of reward. Every week, pundits with sandblasted cheeks and dead eyes breathlessly reported on the latest Patrick Hollen sightings. He was becoming a new bigfoot, it seemed, a crypto-zoological phenomena. There were websites speculating on whether or not he existed, despite some rather obvious and, he'd have though, incontrovertible evidences for the affirmative. Some nutbars out there were constructing a full-blown mythology for him, one that seemed anything but ironic. Pally was, depending on who you asked, a sacrifice, or an example, or a patsy. A patsy for what? Well, plug in your favorite conspiracy theory, and it turned out that Pally had discovered the truth of it and was being eliminated, taken out, *whacked* to help cover it up. It was kind of funny, yeah, but Pally found it hard to laugh about, when there was nobody else was around to laugh with. Or for.

He was losing control of his identity. Hell, who was he kidding; he had *lost* control. His story was no longer his own. A rather banal, unnotable existence (prior to two months ago, natch) had been subsumed by Narrative. He had been given countless Tragic Back-stories – Katie was his second wife, his first having died in a freak skydiving/hang-gliding/competitive eating accident; Lily was adopted, his first child having been snatched by a vulture/turned into a wheelbarrow/executed for treason; Pally himself was a Soviet defector/extraterrestrial stranded on Earth (this one was basically just the plot of *Starman*)/holocaust survivor who had only escaped execution by time travel. He had been given motivations far more grandiose than "free gas for life" – he needed the fuel to take to Puerto Rico to support gureilla campaigns for full statehood; he was hoping to leverage his notoriety into a high-powered job at Tort-Oil, from which he would bring the entire company down and lead a revolution against Big Oil; he was trying to fuel the spaceship he had been constructing in his house to fly back to his home planet. He'd likewise been granted exotic love interests and character arcs and wacky sidekicks and dramatic phone calls and expensive setpieces and merchandising opportunities and sequels and prequels and spinoffs. Pally had ceased to be a person; he had become a product. What would happen when the year was up? What would happen when he sought to reclaim his personhood? Was there anything left to reclaim?

Pally shook his head and found himself, the him that nobody could take (except maybe Gun Guy). Here he was, some number of yards under the surface of Arizona, watching Saul and Margot being cute. Being together. Being happy. Pally sighed and decided, no, it was not time to talk to them. He would be interrupting, and he knew how little he'd have appreciated anybody interrupting Katie and him when they'd been cute, together, happy. So he plopped himself in a chair and waited for Brimley and co. to get back with the free gas that had, in one way or another, ended his life.

24

Turns out it wasn't one way or another – it was one way *and* another. The *how* reached Desert Island via the magic of cable news before Brimley and co. did, so it was Pally who broke the *how* to his host.

"They used the card," he informed Brimley numbly.

Brimley paused from heaving a barrel onto its side and rolling it out the back of the truck. "What's that? *I* used the card. For the gas."

Pally shook his head. "I guess the card had a...Tort-Oil can see when it gets used. So they saw that it got used, and now it's all over the news."

"..."

"I'm really sorry. I don't know why I didn't think of that. Like, of *course* they would do that."

"*You're* sorry? I'm the guy lives underground! I can't figure out I didn't slap that card outta your hand the second I seen it!"

Pally shrugged. "Guess we all do dumb stuff to get free gas."

"Damn." Brimley slapped a hand on Pally's shoulder. "Well, we're really in it together now, ain't we? Bastards. Use it and news it," he chuckled. "Well, alright, let's not *lose* it! That still don't tell your Gun Guy where you are, just the gas station nearest to ya."

"What else is that gas station near?"

"...hm." Brimley finished tipping his barrel and gave it a kick. It ground all manner of grit and grime into the flooring of the van as it rolled towards the lip and *SLAMMED* to the ground, kicking up a plume of sand as it did.

When Pally looked up from the barrel, he saw a new kind of Brimley, set and determined. He stuffed his fingers in his mouth and did that really loud whistle Pally had always wished he could do, but had never quite mastered.

"What's that?" Brenda called.

"Let's clear the barrels double-time and get set! We're gonna have company ain't lookin' to put their dogs up!"

Washington paused, his foot bringing a rolling barrel to a halt. "Pally's Gun Guy?"

"Who else?"

"Sorry, dumb question."

"What a relief I ain't the only fella bein' lunkheaded today! Let's cut the scarecrow shit though, eh? Hup!" Everyone, including Brimley, fell to their labors at once. Still, he shouted in his din-cutting boom as though he *weren't* nudging a barrel of several hundred pounds across the desert, in summer, at high noon. "We ain't sure when he's comin', or even if he's comin', but all the same we gotta account for he *is* comin'."

"We allowed to shoot him?" Brenda wondered, not idly. Pally had regaled them all with tales off the legal wormhole down which the Tort-Oil contract had sent him.

Brimley, however, was non-plussed, and scoffed to demonstrate just how non was his plussedness. "Course we can! ARS 13-406, self-defense is A-OK long as it's reasonable, proportional and immediately necessary. This guy's got 'gun' right in his name, and he'll be trespassin' on our land. Long as he brung his boomstick and holds it where we can see it, whole state of Arizona says 'fire!'"

They finished kicking the barrels down the stairs into the bunker, double-time. Pally helped as best he could, which was not at all, but his eagerness was appreciated. That done, all of the Desert Islanders piled into the living room for a pep talk. As the room filled, Pally shot a look at Brimley. The man was positively giddy, bouncing his knees and fighting the smile that kept sprouting beneath his robust silver mustache. Here was a man who had long dreamt of giving a pre-battle pep talk, Pally realized. This was fun for him. That was probably a good thing; Pally didn't much care what the motivations of his defenders were, as long as they were sufficient for his defense.

"Ok," Brimley boomed once the whole gang had arrived, "we got Gun Guy comin' in for a near certainty. Can't fix on the when or the how, but on that latter score he ain't exactly flush for choice. He can't walk from the two-lane, so its either a car or he's gettin' airdropped in. Latter score of *those* two, we ain't got much recourse 'cept keep ears out for a chopper. Former, we got some options." He pointed to Saul and Margot, who had for once ceased attempting to crawl into each other's mouths. "You two, I'm puttin' top-side. *Separate*," he grinned, which got a knowing laugh from the whole room. Saul and Margot had the decency to laugh and feign frustration, which immediately endeared them to Pally. "You take radios, sunscreen and a hell of a lot of water. Give us a buzz should any sand start blowin' in a way ain't the wind's doin'."

"When do we deploy?" Margot asked.

"Soon as ya can."

Without another word, Saul and Margot sprung from their seats and headed for the door. All business when the chips were down. Pally appreciated that about them too.

Brimley went around the room, pointing to people and assigning them tasks. They all used as much militaristic language as possible, *drum* and *muster* and *billet* and *oh-thirteen-hundred*, and drew a not inconsiderable amount of pleasure from it. It was a fascinating compromise, Pally marveled, between children at play and adults at war. And Hollywood liberal that he was, he was more than happy to avail himself of the fantasies they had dreamt into being, their siege mentality and assault weaponry, even as he stood back and disapproved of the whole production.

Either he was wrong to disapprove, or he was a hypocrite to accept their help. He tended towards the latter, but no amount of highly persuasive statistics on gun violence in the US could trump his craven sense of self-preservation. It was no different than his dietary philosophy: eating meat was, from an environmental and ethical standpoint, largely indefensible. Veganism was all his moral gyroscope steadied for…but what, was he supposed to never eat a pulled pork sandwich again? Not likely. Sorry pigs.

Sorry pigs echoed in his mind as he watched the Desert Islanders gear up and file out.

"What should I do?" he asked Brimley once it was

only the two of them in the room.

"Just keep down here and don't be shot." He handed Pally a radio and slapped him on the shoulder. "I'll give you a ping should I require ya. Otherwise," he added as he grabbed the remote and clicked on the TV, "keep an eye on the news and give *us* a ping if there's somethin' we oughta know."

"Um," Pally pinged. He pointed a finger, which had taken on a hell of a tremble, at the TV.

"What?"

"UM!"

Brimley turned and looked at the TV. "Oh. *Um.*"

A helicopter shot. Gun Guy had driven a semi truck through the chainlink fence, and had taken up position a few dozen yards from the compound's front door. He was prostrate on the far side of a dune, a long-barreled sniper rifle aimed straight for the ingress. At present, he was waving for the helicopter to fuck off, as it was kicking up a whirlwind of sand.

Just then, they heard the whirlywheel on the front door of the compound rattling counterclockwise.

"NO!" they both screamed at the same time.

They heard a loud *splat*, a faint *crack*, and the sound of something heavy *clang*ing down the stairs, something quite a bit softer and more fragile than a barrel of gasoline. Then all they heard was Saul screaming.

On the TV, the tiny Gun Guy instantly lost interest in the helicopter, swiveled to land the stock of his gun on his right shoulder, placed his eye to the scope, and fired. A tiny Margot had just poked her head out the door. Then there was no head and all door.

Sorry pigs, Pally couldn't stop himself from thinking again.

25

Brimley and Pally ran out to the entry stairs. What remained of Margot lay at the bottom in a heap, Saul sprawled on top, weeping into the cavity of her skull. The door at the top of the stairs was still open.

"Jesus Lapedus," Brimley growled as he took the steps two at a time.

"Careful!" Pally shrieked.

As Brimley reached the stop of the steps, the sloping metal wall behind him said *crang*. A flattened bullet tinkled down onto the grating, somehow missing all of the holes and bouncing down to land right at Pally's feet. He crouched down and inspected it. Just a wrinkled little wart of lead. That's all. He glanced at Margot's corpse and thought of pulled pork, and maybe just then converted to veganism. Or maybe he'd never eat again. How could he? There was a death on his hands. Had he never signed up for this stupid contest, had he not come staggering in here looking for help, she'd still be alive.

Having so often looked at her and Saul, and superimposed himself and Katie overtop of them, he couldn't but envisage Katie's face cratered in by a wrinkled little wart of lead (that's all?). Where was Lily in this Boschian frieze? Was she absent for having been secreted away somewhere safe? Or was there another wrinkled little wart of lead (that's *not* all) lying on the ground somewhere, a Desert (Eagle) Island in a rising tide of crimson?

"Sorry pigs," he mumbled to himself. He clapped a hand over his mouth, unable to believe the words had escaped him. Fortunately, there was no way any of the fast-gathering Islanders could have heard him over Saul's wailing. Fortunately.

Looking up, Pally saw that Brimley had taken a seat on the second stair from the top and was waving to everyone below him and shouting "the Kyle! The Kyle!"

The poor man was in shock. "There's nobody named Kyle here!" Pally shouted up to him as Washington thundered up the stairs with one hell of a sniper rifle in his hands. He passed it off to Brimley. Right. The Kyle was a gun. They had names now. Sorry pigs.

Brimley popped out two little legs on the barrel of the rifle and plopped it down on the dirt, pressing his chest into the top step and keeping his head low as bullets cracked into the wall behind him.

Then the world was bells, and Pally was deaf. *Or Pally was deaf.* All was ringing, like Scrooge had just had a change of heart. Only instead of sending the div kid to buy the prize turkey, he had him purchase the entire turkey farm, then liberated them because sorry turkeys.

Sorry div kids.

Sorry Christmas.

Sorry.

Sorry nothing. Sorry didn't do shit. Sorry didn't bring back pigs or turkeys or Margots. That wasn't what apologies were for, bringing things back. Apologies were for futures, not pasts.

Pally stumbled through molasses to dive deeper into the compound, as more shots rang out behind him. He assumed they rang, anyway: he could only recognize them by the way they rattled his chest cavity. He turned and looked.

Brimley wasn't the only one firing out the door now. Grief itself was unsustainable; it demanded a channel. Saul had channeled his into rage, apparently, as Brimley was fighting to keep him from charging headlong out the door, his mouth wide open, thundering a war cry Pally only registered as a shrill ringing.

What would happen when Gun Guy picked them all off? There were no other ways out of here, no windows to climb through, no back doors to jimmy. He was cornered. Sorry Pally.

Thumbs trembling, he dialed up Katie's number. Was it ringing? *Everything* was ringing. He held the phone to his ear and heard nothing. The screen had the little call time counter ticking along, which meant it was connected. Though maybe it had gone to voicemail. No way of knowing.

"I can't hear anything," he said into the receiver. "Hang on."

He pressed the red dot on the screen and saw that he'd had quite a few missed calls over the past few minutes. Some from friends, some from family, most from Katie. He punched open the text window and wrote. He wasn't really sure what he was writing. He was just writing. It seemed highly likely this would be the last communication he ever had with her; it might well serve as his last will and testament.

It would be his Last Word. Even now, in this moment of extremity, he hated himself for being unable to pry his eye from posterity. He wasn't only writing to his wife and daughter, he acknowledged with no small portion of shame, but to the world. He was fully counting on this communiqué being leaked, *somehow*, whether by a cell carrier or the NSA or any of the billions of people he assumed had access to every piece of digitized information about him by now. He watched *Mr. Robot*, after all, and so had adopted an appropriately trendy level of techno-fatalism.

And so his digits flew over the digital keyboard, not a real keyboard but pixels on a screen, arranging letters into words that would serve as adequate facsimiles of real feelings, would *have* to serve, couldn't *possibly* serve. He wrote without thinking; he thought of his wife; he thought of Wolf Blitzer; he thought of his daughter; he thought of Jake Tapper and Rachel Maddow; he thought of Oprah and Ellen; he thought of Charlie Hunnam and Tina Fey; he thought of his parents; he thought of John Irving and Carl Hiaasen and The Foo Fighters and Vitamin Water; he thought of his Vitamin daughter, *water*, no, Lily, like a pad on a pond of Vitamin Water, upon which sat a frog, *The Princess and the Frog.* Sonic the Hedgefrog. *Frog Day Afternoon.* Kieślowski's *Decafrog.* Jimmy Kimmel's nightly monofrog. Andrew Zimmern's gustatory travelfrog. Aaron Sorkin's fast-paced diafrog.

Sorry frogs.

Pally hit 'send' without stopping to see what he'd sent, indeed without even pausing to consider whence his catafrog of amphibian associations. What room was there for a family in a world of frogs? What kind of world allowed frogs to infiltrate so deeply?

He blinked and shook his head. Snapped next to his ears. The ringing was nearly gone.

Stumbling, his inner ear having apparently been just as discombobulated as the listeny bits, Pally made his way back to the entry. He clapped his hands over his ears just in time; more shots slammed through the hall. None of the folks at the top of the stairs had any kind of hearing protection. How?

How indeed?

How...

Something important jostled around in Pally's head. Something obvious. Something as plain to see as that Saul was laying dead halfway down the stairs, unable to return to his lover even in death, or that Brimley's right arm was hanging limp at his side, his shoulder bleeding as Washington tended to it and Brenda took up "the Kyle".

Whatever the important something was, it was disconnected for a moment, and Pally was quite certain he was losing consciousness. Then he was back. His hands had dropped as he'd drifted, though, which meant the ringing was back. Great.

He waddled into the next room and pulled out his phone again. As he swiped his way to a text window for Eric, he glimpsed the last text he'd sent Katie, which, blast it, was now no longer going to be the last text he ever sent, thought maybe that was for the best because the bits that he saw as he swiped through were *i love you all so much, thank you for watching, always root for the underfrog* and *sorry kids.* He also saw that Katie had responded with *Patrick?! What's going on?!*

No time for that now; he opened a window with Eric and fought *very hard* to pay attention to what he was writing this time. *Gun guy just killed two people here. Is that legal?* he asked Eric.

The message sent, and his phone informed him that it was *Delivered* a moment later.

Then the (…) bubble. Oh, how Pally loved and loathed that thing in equal measure.

After an eternity of fifty seconds, Eric replied with a terse *Doesn't look like it.*

So he can be arrested? Pally texted back.

Yes.

Please call police. I can't hear.

Pretty sure the police know. It's all over the news.

Please call anyway.

Ok.

Pally breathed a sigh of relief. It was over. Gun Guy had dug his own grave. What had he been thinking? Did he think that it was suddenly legal for him to kill anybody and everybody, however he wanted? Why wasn't he running? Why…

…

He never did find out how much that contract on his head was worth. How much did this guy stand to make?

Would Tort-Oil pay him no matter what?

Did Gun Guy by chance have a family who could be supported for life, should he make this money? Regardless of whether or not he was in prison?

Were his circumstances, perhaps, dire enough that the prospect of being locked up was less devastating than whatever might happen if he couldn't get this money for a family Pally still wasn't sure existed or not?

What if he had a sick child, and couldn't afford the treatment?

What if he had done a job that had gone wrong, and he had to pay off some real nasty guys if he wanted his family to be left in peace?

What if Gun Guy wasn't some mindless, faceless, nameless killing machine, but a real human being with his own eminently reasonable motivations, who had been pushed into a disreputable trade by circumstance or poor upbringing or what?

Then he was even scarier than before, Pally realized. He'd turned his pursuer into Gun Guy to dehumanize him, to reduce him to a lesser species. It made Gun Guy easy to read: Gun Guy wanted to kill Pally because he wanted money. Simple, thoughtless, dumb. But if he were forced to think of Gun Guy as a person, as a human making difficult choices based not on what was best for *him*, but what was best of *someone else*, even when the latter was incompatible with the former, or even required the negation of the former...

Then Gun Guy, whatever his name was, would keep shooting, keep coming, keep trying to kill Pally until the police physically stopped him. Because he wasn't killing just for money. He was killing for love.

Maybe. Pally didn't actually know whether or not this guy had a family. But surely he'd been coached that killing non-Pallys would mean prison. So this was a decision that he'd made, for *some* reason. That much was certain.

Uncertain: how long would it take for the cops to get here? Where was the nearest town? How many officers did it have? The news crews had scrambled fast, true, but the blood had already been in the water. No way in hell any of them came to Pally's rescue here. This was *Nightcrawler*, this was *Network*. Or it was *The Truman Show*. Or it was some other movie that hadn't been made yet. Rather, it was a movie being made *now*.

Pally ran back to the entryway, hands over his ears. He leapt over the body of Brenda, which had been blasted even further back down the stairs than Margot's.

"GET BACK AND CLOSE THE DOOR!" he screamed. "WE HAVE TO WAIT FOR THE COPS!"

"WHAT?!" Brimley hollered.

"WE ONLY HAVE TO WAIT!"

"I AIN'T WAITIN' ON ANY DAMN COPS!" Washington, who had taken up the rifle, screamed without turning around. Not that keeping his eye on the prize did him much good: a shot caught him at the base of the neck, sent him careening down the stairs.

None of the blood touched Pally. That was all he could think right then. Were this a *real* movie, with proper symbolism and everything, he'd get splattered with some of these people's blood, especially on his hands, which he would then turn over slowly and look at as he reached some kind of grand realization. Maybe he'd realize that the best way to end the bloodshed would be to walk outside and let himself be shot. That would do the trick.

But he didn't want to do that. He shouldn't *have* to. It was so easy! Just close the door and wait! Let Gun Guy drive his semi into it, see if that put a dent in it!

Stan, Yolanda, and another guy whose name Pally seemed to be neurologically incapable of remembering all dashed up the stairs, guns at the ready.

"Wait!" Pally called to them. "The police are on their way! Just wait and th-"

Stan whipped around, his usual five feet away, and pointed his gun directly at Pally's head. "You called the cops? HERE?!"

Yolanda shoved his shoulder. "It's on the news, ya doofus! Cops called themselves! Bridge under the water! Have a good night!"

Shaking his head, Stan lowered his gun and tromped up the stairs. Pally had never imagined one human could point a gun at another and withdraw it with so little ceremony, but then, he'd never met anybody quite like Stan before.

Pally sat on the bottom step, back to the action, and texted Katie again.

Sorry about the last text, he wrote for her, Lily, and nobody else. *I was freaking. Not sure I'm going to get through this. I love you both so much, and I'm so, so sorry pigs.* He very nearly sent it before noticing and removing the *pigs*, chuckling as he did so. If he couldn't managed to get blood on him (which, even as whats-his-name came flying down the stairs, his face flapping in the breeze, was somehow *still* the case), that would have to do for symbolism. That would do, pigs. That would do.

26

Even once he was the last Islander standing, or as the case may have been, laying on the stairs and clutching a limp, blood-soaked arm, Brimley refused to shut the damn door. "This is where rubber and road get to fuckin'," he growled as he delicately nudged Washington's remains off of the rifle and racked it into his left shoulder. "Come up here, I'll need to recruit you on the trigger."

Everything in Pally wanted to say *sure thing* and dash up the stairs. Mr. Agreeable, that was him, always ready with a yes. Well, look where that had gotten him. Stuffed into an underground bunker, surrounded by corpses and somehow, *still*, without a drop of blood on him. That lack of viscera staining his vestments had ceased to be a marvel; now it was just annoying. He was getting off way, way too easy in all of this.

The solution wasn't to be found at the top of the stairs, though. Eight professional, highly trained survivalists had rather dramatically failed to live up to their self-appointed title. How did Brimley imagine he, with his one working arm, and Pally, with his zero steady hands, would fare any better?

"No," the Yes man squeaked.

Brimley quit fiddling with the gun and turned to get a fuller look at Pally. "What did you say to me? In my own damn home?"

"I said, uh, no?" He cleared his throat. "No, I mean? No...?" That uptick in pitch was hard to shake. "That's not the move here, I don't think."

Lifting his arms and grinding his ass into the grating, Brimley shimmied himself around to face Pally. It was a preposterous image, like some weird art installation involving Soviet industrialism and a mustachioed rotisserie chicken. It was a sight Pally might even find funny in a year or two, assuming he still had a brain with which to remember it.

As the gruff would-be drill sergeant turned, Pally saw that the grizzled visage had been reduced to a mask, worn to disguise a deep grief. Imagining a past, a Tragic Backstory, for Gun Guy had put Pally in a reflective mood, perhaps, but he was somewhat certain that what he saw in Brimley's face was a pain of far greater immensity than could be accrued in a single day. Unless, of course, Brimley thought of the Desert Islanders the way Pally thought of this own family...

"Look," Brimley sniffed with a wave of his hand around the entryway. "My men and women, my *friends*, gave their lives protectin' you. We ain't had no reason for that, 'cept the charity-minded hearts we got beatin' in our tits. And you wanna sit there, and t-" Brimley's head exploded. His jaw flew across the room and smacked Pally in the forehead, just as a shower of gore fell upon him.

Ah. *There* was the symbolism.

Should he make it through today, he was going to have to find a therapist, and boy were *they* in for a wild ride. Only, it wasn't just about making it through today. He had to make it through the *year*.

Which he could probably do down here, he realized. They had food. They had water. All he needed to do was *close the fucking door.*

He sprinted up the stairs, loping between bodies with the agility that necessity granted even the least nimble, taking the last few lunges on all fours to keep his head down. He reached the top and peeked over the lip of the highest step.

Gun Guy was sprinting headlong for the door, flat palms cutting the air as he ran. Somebody watched a lot of Tom Cruise movies, then. You know who *else* watched a lot of Tom Cruise movies? Pally. That's how he knew you couldn't run and fire a gun at the same time.

Leaping like, yes, a frog, Pally threw himself over the top step, planted his feet in the dirt, grabbed the latch on the rear side of the door, and leaned back with all of his weight. Gun Guy's face dropped like the ratings of this show would, once Pally got the door closed. Unable to contain his glee, but uncertain of how to manifest it, he stuck his tongue out and gave Gun Guy a little raspberry. Then he remembered the helicopters filming him. Not the most dignified sign-off before a year of solitude, but, ah, fuck it. So he gave the helicopter a little raspberry and laughed.

The door whined and groaned on its hinges, putting up a fight as it neared the frame. Sweat sprouted on Pally's forehead and slid directly into his eyes. He tried to blink it away. Granted, he didn't need his eyes for this bit, but it stung. And now that the door was just about shut, he had the luxury of fretting over such minor things.

Not yet, though. That was premature. The door wasn't closed yet.

Crunch.

The door wasn't closing at *all.*

Pally looked down and found Washington's head between the door and the frame. How had it gotten there? How had he gotten shot and fallen *forward?*

He hadn't, duh. Brimley had pushed him out of the way to get to the gun.

Ah, man.

Pally knew what was going to happen now. Still, he made a, ha, good faith effort to pull Washington's body out of the door, grabbing it by the back of its – no longer *his,* Pally wouldn't be able to handle it so roughly if he thought of it as a *him* – shirt and yanking as hard as he could. Most of it slid out of the door – bits of skull and brain remained. Pally tried closing the door again, but this time it stopped on a *clunk*.

He looked up to see the fat barrel of a gun, the kind of novelty-sized handgun *RoboCop* used, sticking through the door. It didn't have an angle on him, was currently pointing at the wall to Pally's left, but that didn't matter.

He and Gun Guy *both* knew what was going to happen now.

From the world outside, Gun Guy pulled the trigger. The military-grade micropenis compensation device blinded and deafened Pally at the same instant. Bad news was that the sensation of touch was untouched, and so he could feel himself falling backwards, ass-over-end yet again, down the stairs, his fall broken only by the bodies he hit on the way down.

The landing was hard, a flat *splat* on his back. He couldn't breath, but that was fine. He wasn't going to need oxygen for much longer anyway.

No. His new favorite word. *No.*

Yes was the favored word of the defeatist, he decided, blind acquiescence to the will of another. As with all things, it had its place. In moderation, it was a virtue. But moderation could only be achieved when one recognized the vulnerability of the word, the sublimation of the self's desires.

No was power. No was defiance. No was an affirmation of the individual, a denial of the other. As with Yes, No couldn't be treated as an all-purpose Nostrum.

But in the same vein, it was a word of deceptive strength, the muscle of which could bolster the speaker as Atlas held the world. Held, past tense – Pally's world had long since entered free-fall.

Which left it to him, then, to catch it.

"NO," he screamed, without the least interrogatory affectation.

His vision had faded from white to red to black, but he'd regained his ears enough to hear Gun Guy clomping down the stairs, his footfall made heavy by his combat boots on the one hand (or foot), and no doubt a deliberate effort to impress on the other.

"No," Pally sputtered as confidently as he could, laying flat on his back with a mouthful of blood that he couldn't even be sure was his (now that he had blood on him, he was discovering that the symbolism wasn't quite compelling enough to compensate for the yuck factor). "There are no cameras down here. There's no point killing me."

Gun Guy was drawing so close, Pally could hear the creaking of his boots' full grain leather as they shifted through their full range of motion, the chattering of whatever it was he had strapped to his utility belt, the heavy breath he was sucking through his nose to disguise the fact that even Gun Guys got winded by dashes through the desert.

"You're going to jail," Pally informed him, "and you had to know that when you shot those guys. So you're doing this for money, for who? A wife? Kids? Family? Friends?"

Gun Guy's footfalls lost their thin, metallic ring as he passed from the steps to the solid metal paneling of the floor. Something ground beneath his feet, small stones or fragments of bone.

Pally tried to heave himself to his elbows, that he might scoot backwards, but his limbs weren't proving to be especially responsive just then. "They're calling this an entertainment experiment," he wheezed, an unbecoming, plaintive whine creeping into his tone. "You're a part of it too! Did you sign something without knowing what it said too? Did they tr-"

Gun Guy's progress halted. A peephole opened in the darkness, through which Pally could make out a mirage of masculinity swimming in the air before him.

"You signed something," Gun Guy asked in a shockingly delicate baritone, "without reading it first?"

"...yes?"

Gun Guy considered this silently for a moment. "Why would you do that?"

Pally shrugged his shoudlers defensively. "They were really pressuring me. They were like, *you have to sign it.* And I sa-"

"You didn't have a lawyer review it?"

"Well I told them I wanted a lawyer to review it! And they were like, well, they just really wanted me to sign it. And...I just remembered this, the one guy said he was gonna get me a table at a nice restaurant."

"What restaurant?"

"I don't remember."

"What kind of food did they serve?"

"They didn't tell me."

"…what did you order, man?"

"Oh, I didn't ever actually get to go."

Pally could see well enough now to recognize that Gun Guy was shaking his head, like a dad watching his son absolutely whiff a game of tee ball.

Which must have meant, what, that Gun Guy was in some sense invested in Pally? Had he come to identify with his quarry? Here was a chance, then! Like Eric said, the cops were surely on their way here. If he could only keep Gun Guy talking, string him along until they got here…

He still had a chance.

"Listen, what's your name?"

Gun Guy's headshake took on a different quality. "Not for you to know, Patrick."

"That's not fair! You know mine!"

Gun Guy chuckled. "*That's* what strikes you as inequitable about this?"

"Ok, well, answer me this, then, what's a guy who knows words like *inequitable* doing shooting people for a living?"

"Are you implying that contract killers are stupid?"

A perfect example, right here, of a situation in which *yes* was more powerful than *no*. Pally proved the exception to his own rule.

Gun Guy tutted and knelt down in front of Pally. "Ok, well, here's another word for you. *Prejudice*. That's what you've got, buster. You've got a prejudice. Do you know how hard it is, to kill people and get away with it?"

Gassed by defiance, Pally found his elbows and hoisted himself upon them. And, perhaps, a petard of his own making. Oh well; better to have a *somewhat* active hand in one's own demise, rather than take it lying down. Right? "Is this before or after you initiated a standoff in the desert on live television?"

"Why did you say 'in the desert'?"

"…what?"

"That's superfluous information, smart guy. The fact that the standoff happened in the desert is irrelevant to whether or not I've compromised my anonymity."

"…but it happened in the desert. That's where we are."

"That's not relevant to what you were saying though."

"Of course it is!"

Gun Guy crabwalked closer to Pally. Not close enough that Pally could make a grab for his gun, though. Effectively needling an implication though it may have been, Gun Guy was clearly no dummy. To wit: "Here's what I think," he drawled as he did stuff with his gun that made it go *click* and *clack* and just generally make intimidating noises. "And correct me if I'm wrong, because my idiot little hitman peabrain doesn't run at quite the speed of your sign-first-ask-questions-later megacortex. I think that *you* think that police have seen the news and are on their way as we speak, so you're trying to buy time until they arrive by engaging me in inane conversations, and what's more, you're padding those inanities out with as much fluff as you can." He lost interest in his gun and grinned at Pally. "How'd I do?"

"…not bad."

"What do you think are the odds of you having enough head left to hear sirens by the time they get within earshot?"

"…not great."

"Mhm."

"Listen," Pally blubbered, "I have a-"

"Wife and kid?"

"Wife and…yes."

"I know."

Ok, so defiance hadn't worked: how about mewling? "Please, we're where nobody can see us. No cameras, no choppers, nobody." He gestured to the bodies around them. "Half of these are missing their faces. Hell, their *heads*. Take one of them out, tell everybody it's me. I'll stay down here for a year, everything will die down, then I'll sneak out, meet up with my family, and nobody will ever hear anything from me ever again."

"There's a much easier way for me to ensure that last bit."

"Come *on*!" Pally slammed his fist onto the ground. "Ouch! I'm trying to meet you halfway here!"

Gun Guy smiled again. "That's not really how these things work."

"Well, you still have to get me to California, so you can inject me with th-"

"Did you not notice the nine people I shot and killed

on their own property?"

"…"

Goddamnit, why hadn't anybody swooped in to save him at the last second? This was the part where a hole punched through Gun Guy's chest, which he then looked at and said something like "oh, no," then he collapsed and revealed Pally's savior standing up there, silhouetted in the door. Saved from Mr. Silhouette by a Hero Silhouette! How perfect would that be? It would be a rookie cop, or maybe a cop a few days from retirement. Or it would be Brimley, leaning against a wall to attain the stability to fire a gun, injured but, it turned out, not as dead as his missing head might have lead the viewer to believe. Or, somehow, it would be Katie, who had seen the news and come rushing to save him, and she'd picked up a gun from one of the fallen Desert Islanders and nobody knew she would be the hero of the piece but female empowerment was *in* right now, and the only way a male executive could make sense of empowerment was through heavy artillery.

Oh, what was he thinking? This was stupid. None of that would happen until Gun Guy had delivered his final monologue, then said something like "and now, I'm going to kill you," and slowly raised his gun to Pally's forehead, where he would hold it for an inexplicably long period of time.

"Just tell me," Pally begged, knowing full well he had the upper hand here, "since I'm about to die anyway… who are you? Why are you doing this? Why are you willing to go to prison, just s-"

"Mr. Hollen."

"What?"

"You watch too much TV."

"But this *is* TV," was all he could think to say.

"Well," Gun Guy replied as he raised his gun and pressed it in to Pally's forehead, "then consider yourself cancelled."

Pally relaxed; it was only ever the villain who got killed by a one-liner, and since he was the hero of this here st

27

When Katie had agreed to the *Los Angeles Times* interview, she'd failed to truly accept the possibility that her husband would not be giving it with her.

Tort-Oil's production crew had insisted on being in the room when she identified the body, an intrusion against which she fought tooth and nail, ultimately successfully. They had bugged the room with audio equipment, however, and greased whatever skids they needed in order to obtain the security footage. She lear-ned none of this until the airing of the final episode of the three-part documentary *The Shadow of the Pally of Death, sponsored by Zyp*. Mortified, she watched, along with the rest of the world (for the show had proven a hearty success, despite the fact that everybody already knew the ending) as the sheet was lifted from a body that was unmistakably her husband's. The back of his head, she had been informed by a young whitecoat who'd skipped the class on decorum, was "absolutely shredded", but save a small entry hole which the mortician had mercifully covered for the identification, the face was unblemished. After she had watched herself falling to her knees from the cool, omniscient height of a ceiling-mounted fisheye, Katie found it increasingly difficult to access her first-person memory of the experience. This made the fact of her husband's stupid, pointless death both easier, and more difficult, to accept. Not understand, certainly not that, but accept.

Far harder to accept was the hook of the show, the bait that had snagged the kinds of viewing numbers unheard of in the age of five hundred channels and streaming on demand. Somehow, in the name of truth and journalism, or some shit that had even Eric scratching his head, Tort-Oil had received permission from the FCC to run the footage of Pally's execution. Oh yes, they had that footage, because of course Gun Guy (whose name, revealed in the course of his arrest and sentencing, to which he enthusiastically plead guilty, was Greg, fucking *Greg*) had been fitted with a body camera. Which meant that the world, and therefore Katie, were treated to a nipple's eye view of the killing itself. Katie no longer had first-person access to her own experience, yet she now knew what it would have looked like had she herself shot Pally between the eyes.

This was a landmark moment in television, one which occasioned a stupendous amount of conversation, down around the water coolers and up in the ivory towers alike. Scholars philosophized about the subversive commentary the show had smuggled into an ostensibly lowbrow affair, inculpating each and every viewer in the act of violence. Conspiracy theorists pointed out that, given the angle of the shot and the way Greg's (fucking *Greg*, what a name to have listed as the cause of death) arm passed between the lens and Pally's face just before the shot was fired and look freeze it right here now go forward a frame and you can see the stitch, you can see where they cut, it wasn't actually Pally that was shot but an actor, and he wasn't even shot but he was well it was all movie magic like in any other movie. Greg Nicotero, ever heard of him? Yeah, *Greg*. His makeup is *aces*. Others volunteered that the body Katie identified wasn't even a body, it was the wrap cake, which was then wheeled over to a larger room in which the cast and crew (including Pally) all took slices and ate up. Meanwhile, stuffy conservatives shook their heads and tutted at the moral decay rotting the minds of their youth, even as they whispered would you look at the *power* of that, what caliber you think he used? .30-06 mighta been cleaner, but only from a distance. You wanna mount a head, you can't shoot from that close, and anyway, you aim down on the neck or the body, bleed 'em. The airing of the execution footage also served as a convenient scapegoat when the next school shooting happened the following afternoon. Nevermind one had occurred three days before the footage aired, nevermind that this one that followed the airing had been plotted over the preceding weeks;

this wasn't a gun control issue, it was a violence on TV issue!

At first, Katie and Lily were dragged into each and every conversation about this fucking show. They were to be considered co-authors of this treatise; they were in on the cover-up; they were, when you really thought about it, responsible for school shootings. Katie had been offered a reality show a la *The Bachelorette*, in which she would select a new husband. Lily had been offered something similar, though the roses would be handed to those she deemed unworthy of being her new father. This was disturbing, and Katie did her best to shield Lily from the rabid attentions of a seemingly unstable viewer base. In time, though, the conversation detached from them and drifted into pure abstraction. This was a relief in some ways, but in others it was the most disturbing development yet. Indeed, the dialectic surrounding her husband's death seemed to become wholly divested of the subject itself, or at least, his having ever been anything more than a character on a show. People nattered on about his arc, boldly explicating his motivations, making judgments founded on nothing but their own misconceptions about what kind of man Pally was. A few attempts at biography were flung onto shelves, but they didn't sell especially well. Nobody was interested in the real Patrick Hollen. Or rather, the Patrick Hollen that Katie had loved, married and had a child with had ceased to be the real Patrick Hollen. Granted, nobody could agree just who the real Patrick Hollen was, but it sure as hell wasn't anybody Katie had ever met.

So the last thing she wanted to do now, a year and change out from that heart-rending, highly-rated day in the morgue she could only recall as well as anybody else with an internet connection, was to reintroduce herself into the discussion. But she had made a deal, and sticking to it introduced some continuity, as between seasons of a TV show, between her old life, the one that was hers and hers alone, and this new, cloud-based one she was floating through. The interview was exhaustive, the reporter a foreign correspondent who had covered wars and revolutions named Anthony Ryder. She'd expected, and mentally prepared for, a gossip columnist. She wasn't ready for this. The interview was going to be on-camera as well, which she had neither expected nor envisioned when she'd initially made her agreement with a print media outlet. Still, she hadn't explicitly ruled that out, and any continuity she could cobble together, any bridge she could build across the yawning gulf that divided the pre-post- and post-post-Pally parts of her life, was well worth the indignity of the inevitable tearful slow-zoom to which she would be subjected, of which she would be the subject, and so, the object.

No, even a definite article was too much. *An* object. A tearful automaton, playing out her scripted suffering. She, too, was a character.

Ryder pushed to get Lily on camera, but that was a bridge too far. Katie threatened to call the interview off if he didn't drop it. She not-so-secretly hoped that he wouldn't drop it, so she wouldn't have to go through with this. But he did, so she had to.

And so she met the camera crew in their studio, which had been decorated to look like a bog-standard living room (she sure as hell wasn't letting them in to hers), save the framed family photos on the wall. How they had obtained these, Katie didn't know, nor did she care to. They were all real, though. Of that she was sure. Almost sure. People could do incredible things with Photoshop these days, after all. But looking at the photos, she was nearly certain they stirred up memories. And if they didn't, well, now they did. If those memories weren't real, well, now they were.

She sat for makeup, she sat for lighting, she sat and sat and sat until finally they were ready to begin the interview.

"So," Andrew snapped, affording her no more charm or gentility than he had any of the countless dictators whom he had confronted with their crimes, "how does it feel to be this generation's Jackie Kennedy?"

"I wonder what we have in common," she replied coolly, "other than a slain husband."

"Well," Andrew fired back, "you're both telegenic."

Katie laughed until she cried. The camera zoomed in, slowly, slowly.

Also by Jud Widing

A Middling Sort
Westmore and More!
The Year of Uh

If you liked my stupid jokes, you should follow me on
social media @judwiding. I have a lot of them.

94711503R00184

Made in the USA
Middletown, DE
21 October 2018